THE SUICIDE CARTEL

AN AMERICAN MERCENARY THRILLER

JASON KASPER

REGIMENT PUBLISHING

Severn River Publishing

This is a work of fiction. Names, characters, businesses, places, events
and incidents are either the products of the author's imagination or
used in a fictitious manner. Any resemblance to actual persons, living or
dead, or actual events is purely coincidental.

ISBN: 978-1-951249-52-6 (Paperback)

For information contact:

Jason@Jason-Kasper.com

Jason-Kasper.com

To the men of MACV-SOG

THE SUICIDE CARTEL

FORTUNE

Palma non sine pulvere

-No reward without effort

1

September 2, 2009
The Mist Palace
British Columbia, Canada

"Ian, I understand that I'm about to enter a new war. Before I go, what advice do you have for me?"

Ian, an intelligence analyst and my only surviving friend, leaned toward me from across the table. His entire demeanor shifted from nervous to forceful, veins near his balding temples swelling with intensity. Then he folded his hands together as if in prayer, and opened his mouth to speak.

Before he could say a word, the guard standing over us held up his watch and announced, "Four minutes remaining."

I glanced at the guard irritably as he lowered his watch. Neither he nor the other guard made any effort to conceal their eavesdropping, even though they needn't worry about missing a word—black orbs in the ceiling concealed security cameras, and I could only guess what was behind the one-way mirror covering the wall beside us. This level of paranoid security was normal here at the Mist Palace, a secluded wilderness compound serving as the headquarters of a transnational criminal syndicate.

But Ian's intense look drew my attention, and he spoke quickly. "Look, David, there's no easy way to say it, but they're sending you into total chaos, not a war. The Triple Frontier of Brazil, Paraguay, and Argentina is a breeding ground for narcos, terrorists, and gun runners. On one hand you have free-roaming cartel militias securing facilitation corridors. And on the other you have the world's largest population of Lebanese expatriates, so there are Hezbollah training camps in the jungle."

"Sounds cozy," I said.

"There's zero effective border control throughout the zone, and it's filled with unregulated airstrips and waterways. Civilian spotters monitor all of them and report any movement to the cartels."

"Stay away from the rivers. Got it."

"You'll probably run into primitive cocaine labs all over the jungle."

"How well defended are they?"

He shook his head. "They were all decommissioned when the cartels shifted cocaine production out of the area. But trust me when I say those labs are about the only thing you *don't* have to worry about—"

"Three minutes remaining," the guard interrupted.

Ian drew a breath. "Other than that, everything's gotten even worse in the past year. The ongoing criminal war has further destabilized the region. A lot of new players are fighting for a piece of the frontier now that the previous kingpin was ousted by the Handler."

The Handler—the reason for the season, I thought

bitterly. Hell, the reason for everything that brought us here. To the world of high order crime, the Handler was an enigmatic mastermind. He occupied the helm of the ultimate criminal syndicate; he was the king to whom all other criminal fiefdoms bowed.

But to Ian and me, he was a target for revenge.

The Handler had killed our entire mercenary team, the very people who proved to me that even after the military, life had a purpose and my skills had value. Only Ian and I survived. After our botched assassination attempt against the Handler eight months earlier, Ian was enslaved and forced to target the Handler's highest-ranking enemies in South America.

But I'd just turned all that around by negotiating Ian's freedom. We'd only been granted a few minutes together before being separated forever. A private jet would whisk Ian away to spend the rest of his life under passive surveillance, while I would be shipped to the war in South America.

Every word of our final minutes together would be scrutinized by the Handler's intelligence agents. Ian knew that better than I did, as well as the harsh reality that if he said anything remotely suspicious, the deal for his newly-won freedom would be null and void. And yet, Ian's body language and expression told me he was about to pass along a coded message, something that everyone would hear but only I would understand. He was smarter than they were, and he knew it.

I just had to pick out the clues—but I'd heard nothing so far besides information I'd surely receive later in a mission brief. Was Ian laying trivial groundwork for the real code?

But Ian's tone switched from informative to almost

wistful as he continued, "You know, David, now that my career is over, I've been thinking a lot about the past. When you and I worked together on Boss's team, it was a golden era. We were one of a dozen or so teams handling mercenary work at any given time. But all that changed after Boss's last mission."

I nodded distantly, thinking of our team's final job for the Handler. We'd delivered mission success in the form of a decapitation strike against his US-based criminal opposition.

And for our efforts, the Handler had us massacred.

The memory elicited a tumult of conflicting emotions in me—grief for Boss's team, rage at the Handler, a desolate sadness that my last surviving team-mate was about to walk out the door, and I'd never see him again.

Ian shook his head. "Made me sad to think all those teams are gone now. And then, David, I realized that they're not."

I frowned at him. But those teams *were* gone now, and everyone knew that. Many had fled the country, especially after a few of their fellow mercenaries inexplicably went missing. Other teams, like the one Ian and I served on, had been killed before being able to escape the Handler's wrath.

I rubbed my forehead and replied, "I don't understand. What do you mean, those teams aren't gone now?"

There was a gleam in his eye as he leaned in to explain, "Don't you get it? Boss's team is still alive, in us. You and I carried the torch to the end."

"Yeah, I suppose so," I agreed reluctantly. "As far as that type of work goes, I'd say this moment is the definition of the bitter end."

The guard announced, "Two minutes remaining."

Ian still appeared to be fondly reminiscing as he asked, "Remember the first mission you did for Boss?"

If Ian had already passed a coded message, then it had sailed cleanly over my head—or was I wrong? Maybe he didn't have a message at all. Perhaps I'd misread him completely, or he was just going batty after his long months of indentured servitude.

I nodded. "My first mission—assassinating Saamir. Of course."

He shot me a knowing look. "Since I've been working here at the Mist Palace, I've been having dreams about Saamir. That he's hiding out in his office, still alive."

"I recall killing him pretty clearly, but okay."

"I didn't get it either, until today. This morning I realized why I've been having these dreams. When security found out you were inside Saamir's building, Boss thought it was too dangerous for you. He ordered you to abort the mission. But you disobeyed. Against all odds, you shot your way to the roof to parachute off and escape."

My eyes were locked on his, waiting for some emphasis that didn't come.

"Hard to forget, Ian."

"The time between those two events—you disregarding Boss's order to abort, and then actually freefalling off the roof—was the most scared I've ever been for an operative. In hindsight, it was the most memorable moment of my career."

"Glad I could contribute," I offered, trying to leave an opening for Ian to speak further. "Anything else I need to know about South America?"

"One minute remaining," the guard called.

Ian gave an almost parental grin at my impatience. "The most important part. No matter how bad things get

5

—it's an ugly war, David—keep hope. If you could blow off a mission abort and still come out of Saamir's building alive, then you can make it back from South America." He leaned back in his chair with a satisfied expression and folded his hands across his belly. This wasn't the end, I thought. This *couldn't* be the end. Not of the message, and not of my time with a friend I didn't want to leave.

I nodded helplessly. "I got it, but—"

"I won't be able to help you," he cut in, "but you don't need me anymore. Remember that."

"Time's up," the guard called. He and his partner grabbed Ian's wiry frame and hoisted him upward.

I leapt up from my chair. "You motherfuckers—"

Ian put up a hand to stop me. "Don't worry about me, brother. You've got a war to win."

The guards forced him toward the door. My last sight of his face revealed a smile and a wink as he yelled over his shoulder, "You will get out of this, David."

Oh, how the tables had turned.

Eight months ago I'd returned from Rio de Janeiro and managed to smuggle a weapon into the Handler's garden with the full intention of assassinating him. But when I instead found Ian a bound captive, I utilized that weapon to spare my friend's life.

And just before the Handler's men separated us, taking Ian to a cell and me into a deep cover assignment almost certain to end in my death, my last words to him were, "I will get you out of this, Ian."

I'd now made good on that seemingly hopeless promise by securing Ian's release. In return he'd just fed my own words back to me, presumably indicating I was headed into a trap myself.

But what was it?

A wave of despair crashed over me as I lost sight of

Ian, the guards whisking him down the hall and letting the door slam in their wake. After Ian and I survived the decimation of our team, after we'd come so close to avenging them in a year-long journey, he was gone and I was left behind, truly alone.

2

_____

After being locked in my bedroom for the night, I paced the small room like a caged animal.

In a way, I was.

It was the same room where I'd been kept earlier that year, rehabilitating from surgery to repair a trio of gunshot wounds. Surely glamorous accommodations existed somewhere in the secret compound, but this room certainly wasn't one of them.

Mine was more like a second-rate hotel room, though here I had no control over the keypad-controlled deadbolt whose code was unknown to me. I didn't even know my location within the confines of the Mist Palace—I was always transported to and from this space while blind-folded and under guard.

Now I'd be alone until the following morning, when the Handler would fly me to South America to meet my new mercenary team. We'd be off to wage war against the Handler's enemies, an assignment I'd requested—but the long night ahead of me would be unbearable.

I was plagued by mental claustrophobia, my thoughts

swarming in a bar brawl fight to decipher Ian's message. Or was there anything to decipher? His facts about the Triple Frontier were surely true at risk of the Handler's people catching him in a lie—but what about the rest? Why reference Boss, or my assassination of Saamir? He'd said nothing that couldn't be fact-checked there, either. The Handler had quoted my dead teammates during my Outfit interview, proving what I'd later been told—our team house was under surveillance the entire time.

A sudden spike of pain ran up my spine, forcing me to stop pacing and sit on the bed. I lay sideways on the mattress, shifting uncomfortably to prevent the full-body ache from intensifying.

The source of pain was obvious enough.

When Ian was imprisoned eight months earlier, the Handler forced me into service as a deep cover agent. My mission was to uncover a disloyal operative, who turned out to be a beautiful redhead named Sage. She was an assassin and seductress of such skill that she alone stood capable of outsmarting and killing the Handler.

And that's exactly what she'd tried to do.

To say that Sage had rescued me would be truthful but misleading. In this bizarre criminal underworld, she saved my life only by faking my death. I'd been a willing disciple to her assassination plot up until the bitter end, when I discovered that she intended to detonate the Handler's nuclear device amid thousands of innocent people in Rio de Janeiro. It took considerable effort to dismantle her coup, and even more to kill her. I was quite handy with a gun, but she was a trained martial artist and quickly disarmed me.

Now, my body still ached from the hilltop battle that ensued—one that had very nearly killed me. But in the end I'd cheated to win, using a poisoned pen to kill Sage. In the process I'd saved the Handler's life, earned Ian's freedom, and been assigned a mercenary team to lead in South America.

I rolled to my side on the bed, tucking my hands beneath my head in a failed bid to get comfortable. The physical pain was, as usual, bearable. But far worse than the bruises and welts from hand-to-hand combat was the scene that unfolded in the Handler's court upon my return. I could happily endure the judgment and hatred of him and his executive staff, but when his daughter Parvaneh entered, it took everything I had not to beg her forgiveness.

She had fallen in love with me after I saved her life in Rio, but that sentiment cooled considerably upon her discovery that I was her father's would-be assassin. Moments later, when she found out that my former mercenary team had mistakenly killed Roshan, her fiancée and the father of her daughter, any love Parvaneh felt toward me turned resolutely to hate.

She was unable to even look at me in the courtroom, and her resentment had turned my participation in the upcoming war in South America from a career move into a welcome reprieve.

The thought of Parvaneh made me restless, and so I heaved myself up from the bed and began to pace once more. Checking my watch, I saw that I'd scarcely been in the room for an hour.

I forced my mind back to Ian's message as I walked back and forth, turning on my heels when I reached the wall. His dream that Saamir was alive in his office—what had that meant? And why had he tried to assure me that I could return from South America alive?

I had to figure it out—if I didn't, the Handler's people would.

Or maybe they already had.

Suddenly I heard the clatter of the keypad outside my door—someone was opening my cell, a process that inevitably ended in me being transported like a prisoner. The armed guards, the handcuffs and blindfold, the visionless shuffle to wherever they were leading me next.

But no one was scheduled to get me until morning.

They'd figured out something in Ian's message, I realized, and were coming to take me away. The deal was broken, or the Handler had simply changed his mind.

The door swung open and closed with alarming quickness, a single tall figure sweeping inside my room in the interim.

Parvaneh.

Her electric green eyes met mine as she stood before me.

She made no move to advance further, though I could reasonably guess why she had come. I looked to her hands—to my surprise, they were empty.

"If you want my life," I said, "you can have it."

"I'm not here to hurt you. I came alone, and in secrecy."

I almost laughed in her face. "There are no secrets here. No one walks around the Mist Palace unnoticed."

"No one," she said, with a confident smile, "except me."

"What about the guards, the cameras?"

"I have my own way around those."

"That's impossible."

"I'm the only one who has seen this place through the eyes of a child."

I shrugged. "Meaning...what?"

"Meaning no one is aware that I am here."

I remembered Sage's description of the fort's exhaustive defenses and security protocols, and felt at my core that no such secret route existed. It was simply inconceivable.

I asked, "Then why have you come?"

She cleared her throat uneasily. "You hadn't yet met your team when they killed Roshan."

"I told you that in your father's garden."

"I was...wrathful when my father confronted me with your past. I have a dark side, David, one that is, at times, difficult to suppress. When I left the garden, I took one look at my daughter Langley and realized how wrong I was. I became despondent that my anger overcame the bond we had in Rio, and I tried to reverse your assignment against Sage."

"The Handler made sure it was too late for that, I'm sure. He signed the operation into existence as soon as we left the garden."

"Of course. And when I heard you were killed..." Her eyelashes fluttered as she blinked back tears.

"Sage said you ripped my death report out of her hand before she could even submit it."

"This is true. But I did so out of regret for my complicity. I mourned you, David. And Sage knew that as well as anyone. Finding out you were alive changed everything for me...I couldn't even look at you in your court proceedings out of fear that I'd cry."

I stepped toward her, taking her hands in mine. "You can look at me now."

But she didn't. Pulling her hands away, she began unbuttoning my shirt instead.

I watched her closely, trying to discern her intent. It

wasn't seduction, but I didn't understand what she was doing until she slid the shirt off my left side.

Her fingers caressed my left shoulder and deltoid, and then swept across to my right shoulder—all scarred.

"These are from you getting shot to save me in Rio?"

I nodded. "And the surgery afterward. Fractured humerus, fixed with some titanium plates. All in all, a pretty simple fix."

She stripped my shirt off the rest of the way, and then looked lower on my left side.

"What about these?"

I looked down to the two nearly identical circles of raised pink flesh on my bicep and ribs.

"Souvenirs from my job interview for the Outfit."

Her eyebrows drew together in a pained expression. "Who did this to you?"

"Some sick bastard who works for your father. I don't know his real name. I called him Cancer."

"Are you proud of your scars?"

I was taken aback by her question.

"Proud? No. They're just...the cost of doing business. They're nothing."

I knew she'd ask about the bruises next. The evidence of my hand-to-hand combat with Sage was mottled across my upper body.

But instead, Parvaneh ran a hand across the side of my head, tousling my hair. "What about these scars? The ones that no one else can see."

I took her hand and lowered it. "Are you suggesting I have psychological issues as a result of prolonged exposure to combat, Parvaneh? I've never heard of such a thing."

Smiling, she pulled her hand away. "On our flight back

from Rio I offered you a seat on my delegation." She fixed her eyes on mine as her face grew solemn. "When you return from South America this time, I want you to take it."

"I don't think your father will allow that."

"Let me worry about my father. You just worry about returning from this war in one piece, and I'll take care of the rest."

"I'm not a diplomat, Parvaneh. Or a negotiator. I don't know how much use I'd be on your delegation."

"You've got a good heart, David. I can teach you everything else." She stroked my hair again. "And the human mind's capacity for pain is not infinite. I want you to step out of combat and begin to heal. Besides"—her lips slid into a grin—"if nothing else, you could be a bodyguard. You've saved my life once. I'm quite sure you could do it again."

I took a breath, contemplating the offer. "After I return from the war, consider me hired."

Her lips parted slightly for a moment of disbelief. "Really?"

"I've had some close calls to date. My number will be up soon if I don't step off the path. Besides, I'd like to spend more time with you. You seem to have a calming effect on me."

"More than Sage?"

"Too soon, Parvaneh."

She pushed a tendril of hair away from her eye, speaking quickly. "I'm not jealous, it's just that—"

"If you want to know, I'll tell you."

"I know what she was, David. You don't have to tell me."

I nodded, remaining silent until she spoke again.

"Did you know that I got a scar in Rio, too?"

"No." I looked over her sections of exposed skin. "When?"

"During the initial ambush, when you got out of the car. It must have been a splinter from a bullet or something."

"Could be. Where did it get you?"

She began unbuttoning her shirt, exposing her white bra and the long, lean abdomen below it. I thought back to when we changed clothes in the favela in Rio, to seeing her undress just as she was doing now.

Tossing her shirt on the bed, she turned a hip to me and pressed a finger to her side, just above a hint of lace extending above her waistline.

"Here," she said.

Kneeling, I squinted at the spot, then shook my head. "I think that's a birthmark."

"Look closer."

Leaning forward, I kissed her warm skin. She put her hand on the back of my head and pulled me in, a soft gasp escaping her lips.

She led me to the bed and then straddled me as our mouths met. She was slow and tender, and we made love for the most elated period of my life. All pain was gone— from my body and my mind. The chronic sufferings of combat and physical abuse and psychological trauma were replaced with tender intimacy and a wholly fulfilling closeness of human contact. Some spiritual dimension within me, long since dormant and thought lost, was reawakened with vibrant energy.

I watched her from the bed as she got dressed, her face glowing with subtle satisfaction.

Her last words to me were, "Happy hunting, David Rivers. Come back to me safe."

Without waiting for a response, she spun and

approached the door, pausing for a moment before entering a code into the keypad. A quiet beep preceded a deadbolt sliding open before she pushed the door open and stepped outside.

The door eased shut behind her, allowing me a glimpse of her form cutting left in the night before the heavy lock clacked back into place.

3

September 5, 2009
Foz do Iguaçu, Brazil

An Outfit support guy picked me up from the airport in Foz do Iguaçu, delivering me to my team's safe house as the sun was just beginning to crest the horizon.

I exited the car, noting the air had a hint of chill to it—probably sixty degrees, I guessed, but that was before sunrise. The coming day would be swelteringly hot.

I glanced about as I unloaded my bags from the trunk, finding the neighborhood to be comprised of townhouses behind green iron fences. A man stepped out from the nearest gate to help with my bags—and to my surprise, I recognized him at once.

"*Sua Sponte*, motherfucker," he said, walking forward to shake my hand. His frame was large and well-muscled, though his face—and voice—were boyish, almost child-like in their enthusiasm.

"Now there's a familiar face." I shook his hand, adding, "Never thought I'd see you again, Reilly."

He took one of my bags and escorted me toward the

house, locking the gate behind us.

"You can say that again," he almost laughed, leading me through the front door. "One minute we're discussing the ladies of Rio—"

"I think you were the only one discussing the ladies of Rio."

"—the next, I jump off the chopper and find you lying in a pool of blood and the traitor with his face blown off. The ambassador you saved was trying to stop your bleeding, but she had about as much knowledge of trauma medicine as I do of fidelity."

As he walked me into the safe house, I had an eerie sense of déjà vu—one that, I quickly decided, was attributable to Boss's team house. Both bore the hallmarks of being occupied by a group of men, devoid of any feminine influence: worn furniture; scarred floors; dusty, cobwebbed corners. Dishes in the sink yet a neat alignment of liquor bottles on the countertop.

Even the layout of rooms seemed similar, and as I glanced out the sliding glass door behind the chipped dining table, I half-expected to see the overgrown yard leading to the backwoods range where Boss's team had trained me to kill Saamir.

Instead I saw a cluster of banana trees framed by a brick perimeter wall, leaving me to wonder how much of the similarity had been my imagination.

Reilly continued, "So after I saw you last, how'd you do at...uh, your destination?" He was referring to the Mist Palace, any mention of which was strictly forbidden among the Outfit. That rigid law hadn't stopped Reilly from openly discussing the Handler's inner sanctum with me when we were last alone in Rio—he must have been obeying protocol not for my benefit but for that of someone else in the house.

"Sorry, I can't tell you much," I replied, matching Reilly's guarded phrasing. "Special assignment. Compartmentalized project."

Reilly nodded, indicating that my vague response was a wise one. I made a mental note that a true Handler loyalist must be among the team here.

And turning the corner of the downstairs hallway a moment later, I saw him.

He was tall with a lean build and flecks of gray in his hair. He addressed me with a trace of Latino accent that I remembered well. "Hello again, David."

I grinned, incredulous, accepting his hand and shaking it.

"Hey, Sergio. They send you down to supervise me or what?" I asked. He looked much as he had the last time I'd seen him at the Outfit airfield, just before I went to the Mist Palace for the first time, though I noticed that his eyes now harbored the darting alertness of a man recently removed from combat and his previously manicured goatee was now a sprawling beard.

Sergio shook his head. "I'm on the team. As your second-in-command."

I tried not to appear surprised—he'd recruited me into the Outfit, had prepped me for my meeting with the Handler, and was easily my senior by a decade if not more. He'd also been a little more than upset when I'd been allowed to meet the Handler, a privilege he'd never received. Was his assignment here intended to slight him further, or serve as an obstacle for me?

Before I could muster a response, he pointed into a bedroom. "Your room. Just set your stuff in there for now; we'll get everything set up when we get back in thirty-six hours."

"Get back from where?"

"Reilly didn't tell you? Change of mission came in a few hours ago. We're about to blow out on an operation."

Reilly and I set my bags down inside the room. My eyes were drawn to the bed, which was covered in tactical kit—a chest rig with magazine and grenade pouches, and a suppressed M4 assault rifle with optic, infrared laser and tactical light.

That much was to be expected, as was the assortment of field rations, water bladders and canteens, a radio with spare batteries, and clothing.

But a staggering amount of ammunition was present as well. I counted fourteen thirty-round rifle magazines lined up across the mattress.

"Holy shit," I muttered. "Double combat load?"

Sergio nodded. "This isn't Afghanistan, David. No resupply bird is going to swoop in if we shoot our load in one gunfight. We've got no support until exfil."

This rucksack was going to be enormously heavy, I thought with a sense of dread. And I hadn't even counted the explosives—five fragmentation grenades and two Claymore anti-personnel mines. One was in a bandoleer with the usual components: hand-operated firing device and enough wire to allow the user a safe distance when he activated it.

The second mine was rigged with a device I recognized but had never seen issued: a non-electric firing system with a time delay.

I pointed to it. "What's the time delay on that Claymore?"

"Sixty seconds. If we need longer than that, we'll have a chance to adjust the time setting. Everyone's carrying the same load, save some specialty kit."

"How many guys on our team?"

"Counting you and me, we've got five. Reilly's our

medic, Alan's our sniper, and Viggs is our communications guy."

"Viggs," I said thoughtfully, unable to place the name. "Why does that sound familiar?"

Sergio smirked. "You'll see. Come on upstairs, we'll start your mission brief."

Reilly and I followed him up the steps. The last time I'd addressed Sergio, I was a throwaway operator intent on trading my life for the Handler's within the next ten minutes. Sergio had borne keen witness to my youth, my cynicism, my frivolous disrespect of the Organization and its leader—both of which Sergio held dear. I may as well have slandered his religion, and now he was expected to obey and advise me as team leader.

We entered a bedroom that had been modified into a planning bay—laptops and computer monitors haphazardly rigged across tables, one wall left open for a projector to cast mission briefs before an audience of empty foldout chairs. Black cloth had been pinned over the windows, preventing outside view.

A huge bald man was hunched over one of the computers. He turned as I walked in and stood quickly, looking hesitant, as if trying to gauge my reaction to his presence.

Sergio smiled. "David, this is Viggs. Our radio operator."

Momentarily taken aback at the sight of him, I tried to appear casual as I shook his hand.

"Viggs," he said.

"I remember. David."

It was a struggle to remain professional. Viggs had beaten me before tossing me into freezing water to drown —but that was part of the Outfit selection process, I reminded myself. And in his defense, I'd started a fight with him by trying to break a beer bottle over his head. Besides, it wasn't like he was the guy in the basement who put out cigarettes on my flesh.

My first partner in the Outfit told me that if I worked there long enough, I'd one day be a part of running that sadistic selection process myself. Viggs probably didn't have a choice in the proceedings, and were we to switch places, neither would I.

Clearing my throat, I tried to defuse the tension. "How delightful to see you again. Better circumstances this time."

"'Course. This type of reunion happens all the time in the Outfit, hope you understand—"

"Forget about it. If you can fight in the jungle anything like how you can fight in a bar, then we're all in good hands." I briefly wondered if the Outfit selection process was designed to pit us against one another from the start, maintaining internal dissent among Outfit shooters so we couldn't rise up against the Handler.

"I'm even better in the jungle," Viggs assured me. "Wait till you meet Alan—he's on his way back from coordinating our infil at the departure airfield. The guy's an Outfit legend. Three cash bonuses for valor in this current campaign alone, and that's the least of his accomplishments."

"Great."

"Extremely accomplished sniper. Need target overwatch or a long-range shot? He's your guy. And he'll run to the sound of guns like no other."

Sergio interrupted, "David, please have a seat. We need to get you up to speed on the mission that just came down. Transport leaves for infil in three hours."

I took a seat in one of the foldout chairs as Viggs

prepared the projector. Sergio stood beside the blank wall, ready to start his briefing.

"Glad we're not wasting any time," I said. "What's the infil platform?"

Sergio replied, "Helo. And a bit of a walk to our target."

"Great. Who are we killing?"

"We're, ah, we're not killing anybody. It's a recce mission."

"Reconnaissance? Of what?"

"Intel hit on a possible hiding spot for some of Ribeiro's second-tier executive staff. If we're lucky, people high enough to know which country—or continent—Ribeiro fled to. We need to confirm or deny if they're present."

"But if they are, we can bang the target, right?"

"Negative. There's a direct-action force repositioning within strike range now. Once we infil, they've got priority of assets in case there's a follow-on objective."

Reilly took a seat beside me, and I glanced from him to Viggs.

Then I asked, "You guys been running recon together this whole time?"

Viggs answered, "We haven't been running anything together."

My face went slack. "I don't follow."

"We were all operating separately before that. Sergio was advising host nation mercenaries in Venezuela on account of him speaking the language. Reilly was on a unilateral Outfit team operating in Colombia. Me and Alan were both recce between Brazil and Bolivia, so we've got the most recon experience in this area, but we were on separate teams before this."

I folded my arms, troubled. "So they pulled everyone

from four different countries and threw you together as a team...when, exactly?"

"Three days ago."

Exactly when the Handler had granted my request to lead an Outfit team in the war.

"Why'd you guys get pulled together?"

Viggs shrugged. "Said they needed to stand up a new team and were shipping down a fresh Outfit leader to run it. We were supposed to be a direct-action element, but the intel tip is across the border in Argentina, and we're the closest unassigned people. So they said suit up for recon and get eyes on while they stage the assault force."

Only then did I realize an uncomfortable truth, one that explained exactly why the Handler had met my demand of leading a team in the war, even against the counsel of his Chief Vicar of Defense. It had been too easy, I thought, and now I knew why. These men were too diverse an assemblage to be randomly selected. The Handler didn't do things by accident, so what was the meaning of this? I could conjure only one answer, but it was a good one: I was being set up for failure.

Any three Outfit guys would have been pissed about the arrival of a twenty-six-year-old kid nominated as their military superior. So the Handler had arranged two people that would maximize this friction—Viggs, who had tortured me during my Outfit selection, and my former boss Sergio. I couldn't similarly explain the presence of Reilly, who was affable enough and had even rescued me after I was shot in Rio. But Reilly's assignment may have been more pragmatic: we needed a medic if we were going to tiptoe around the jungle with no outside support.

Before I could consider this further, the wall before

me blazed into a map of the Triple Frontier as the projector magnified the laptop display.

"All right," Sergio announced. "Let's get started with the mission brief. As far as criminal and terrorist organizations are concerned, the Triple Frontier is situated neatly at the fissure line of governance between three countries." He waved a finger at the map. "Throw in a massive Arab population and a few drug cartels, and you've got the perfect fusion of terrorism and crime. Safe haven, training, and trafficking are the norm, and that's before we get into money laundering that runs in the billions each year. But for the purposes of today's mission, we'll focus on ground threats. Slide."

Viggs punched a button on the keyboard, and the image shifted from an overhead map to a diagram depicting the size of enemy forces.

"Cartel activity is a crapshoot," Sergio quipped. "Multiple players swarming in to fill the gap with the fall of Ribeiro's organization. Our infil route is away from suspected facilitation corridors, but we could easily encounter up to a platoon-size force of cartel militia. And the massive Lebanese population makes it a hub for Hezbollah. We've got unconfirmed reports of terrorist training camps in the jungle."

Not so unconfirmed—Ian had told me there were definitely Hezbollah camps here.

I asked, "What can we expect from Hezbollah? How many men, how many camps?"

"If the training camps are even there?" Sergio asked. "No one knows. Western intelligence hasn't been taking the region too seriously outside of urban population centers. But the Intelligence Directorate advised us on the presence of spotters and early warning networks protecting enemy interests and likely watching waterways for any activity." Another point for Ian's information, I thought.

Sergio turned back to the projection of the Triple Frontier. "Vegetation density is variable, mostly based off proximity to water sources. In the densest areas, enemy forces pass each other on separate trails only meters apart, not realizing the others' presence. In other spots, it's possible to see, and be seen, at distances up to a hundred meters. With good fieldcraft, we can expect to bypass any enemy forces we encounter. Questions so far?"

"None," I answered.

"Slide." The display changed to an overhead satellite view of rolling jungle. A red arrow hovered over an otherwise unremarkable spot marked by a six-digit grid.

"Our target is a suspected building cluster, the emissions source for several intercepted satellite communications. The objective rests under triple canopy, necessitating reconnaissance by a ground team. Slide."

Viggs flipped the image to an overhead view of the Triple Frontier with four points marked across the border in Argentina.

"Infiltration," Sergio continued, "will be plus or minus three hours from now—"

"*Daytime* helicopter infil?" I asked.

"That's the norm around here. The largest waterfall system in the world is at the border of Brazil and Argentina."

"Iguazu Falls," Reilly said, as if that should be obvious.

Sergio nodded. "Continual helicopter passes each day carrying tourists. Any aircraft flying at night is assumed to be police or military. So we'll launch this afternoon, flying the tourist route up to the border. A decoy chopper will fly our route back to the departure airfield while we cross into Argentina."

Then he pointed to four boxes marked on the map, tapping them in sequence as he spoke. "Possible fast rope points—Primary, Alternate, Contingency, and Emergency. Papa, Alpha, Charlie, Echo. If we see any activity at our primary, we've got three bumps before we have to re-cock for alternate infil. If we take contact before fast-roping, it's your call on whether to divert infiltration point or return to base. Slide."

The projector display flipped to dismounted patrol routes that led from each of the four infiltration points toward the objective. The landscape was shown in mottled contour lines delineating the slope, and each hilltop was marked with a two-digit identifier to facilitate navigation.

"Dismounted movement will be two to three kilometers, depending on where we infil. We'll walk as far as we can before sunset today, and then bed down for the night. At sunrise we'll hump the remaining distance to our objective, attempting to get eyes-on no later than 2300 tomorrow. Viggs, cover the comms."

The slide flipped to communications, and Viggs began reciting radio frequencies, reporting procedures, and then —catching me by surprise—call signs.

"Team call sign is 'Tomcat.' David is 'Tomcat Actual.' Sergio is—"

The hair on the back of my neck stood up. "Who chose that designation?"

Viggs looked confused. "It's assigned. Outfit teams go by cats, our support elements are dogs..."

I thought back to my previous Outfit missions. In Somalia, our call sign was Bobcat. In Rio de Janeiro, we were Jaguar.

"I get that," I said. "But who chose 'Tomcat' specifically? Our Outfit chain of command or someone in the Organization?"

Sergio cut off Viggs's response.

"We don't know, and it doesn't matter. Viggs, go on."

Viggs kept speaking, but I barely heard him. The source of that call sign mattered a great deal. In Rio de Janeiro I'd obtained a tiny .32 pistol that I smuggled toward the Handler—quite unsuccessfully, it turned out —to use during the assassination.

A Beretta 3032 Tomcat.

Viggs finished briefing his communications protocol, and the slide flipped to a wire diagram of the enemy organization. Reilly began reading names from a notebook, starting with the highest leader.

Ribeiro was easily identifiable thanks to our brief meeting in Rio de Janeiro earlier this year—portly Latino features amplified by the cartoonish addition of thick lenses that made his eyes appear froglike.

Ribeiro's photograph sat atop the pyramid of a wire diagram descending into a complex array of executive staff. I scanned the portraits, searching for one that I knew I'd find in the organizational structure.

Agustin.

His beard was shorter than I remembered, but his eyes held the same air of thoughtfulness and compassion that matched his voice during our single conversation—an appearance that had deceived me completely.

I stabbed a finger at the photograph. "This gentleman right here. Who is he?"

Reilly checked his notebook. "Agustin Villalba. Operations officer."

"Operations officer...for Ribeiro's entire organization?"

"Yes." Reilly nodded as he flipped a few pages and read the notes before continuing. "Looks like he was deputy ops, and took over when his boss got promoted to Ribeiro's executive officer last year."

"What else do we know about him?"

"Nothing. He's a second-tier objective, likely left behind when Ribeiro fled the region, probably for North Africa."

"Good. Then we'll have a chance of killing Agustin."

Sergio cocked his head. "You know him from your Rio delegation?"

"He talked to me about his faith, about the Christ the Redeemer statue we could see out the window. A few hours later he led a team into the favela to kill us all—and the fact that he was operations officer means he was there because he enjoyed it. I smoked his team, but Agustin was the one that got away. Literally and figuratively." I cleared my throat. "I owe him a debt I intend to repay."

Viggs protested, "We're not likely to encounter him if—"

"If we do, Agustin is mine."

Sergio quickly redirected the conversation, and I kept quiet as Reilly finished his brief on the enemy command structure. Then Viggs flipped the slide to mission contingencies.

Reilly's phone chimed a text. He checked the display and announced, "Alan's back. I'll go let him in."

"I'll get him," Viggs interrupted, rising and leaving the room before Reilly could object.

Sergio released a loud breath. "Contingencies. In the event of enemy contact, we execute a break contact drill, run two to three hundred meters, and then begin evasive maneuvers. Dropping rucks is a last resort. In the event the enemy captures one of us, we are not to speak a word. Moving on to—"

"Wait a minute," I stopped him. "What do you mean,

we're not to speak a word?"

"Correct. Standard Outfit protocol."

I looked to Reilly. "Either of you been captured before?"

They both shook their heads.

"Well I have," I continued, thinking of my tortured captivity at the hands of Myanmarese soldiers, "and keeping quiet isn't really an option. You wouldn't even live long enough to attempt escape or await a rescue."

Sergio cut in, "That's the point, David. Total mission closure. No one comes to rescue Outfit operators."

"But they'd sure as shit send us to our deaths to rescue an ambassador, wouldn't they? Well as long as I'm in charge, none of us are expendable. If you're captured, you buy as much time as you can and attempt escape. Tell the enemy whatever you need to."

Sergio shook his head curtly. "Outfit men are expected to keep silent and sacrifice our lives for the Organization. It's what our selection process screens us for, David—the ability to resist divulging secrets, all the way to the grave."

I sat back in my seat, enraged. Why have such an inane policy? It signified everything I hated about the Organization—reducing its servants to animals, condemning them to death and removing any possibility of surviving and returning home with their honor intact.

I didn't get a chance to continue the debate as I heard the sound of two people climbing the steps.

Viggs walked into the briefing room first, then stepped aside to make way for a second man.

Our final team member looked too old to be carrying the suppressed SR-25 sniper rifle held lightly at his side. The last time I'd seen him holding that same rifle was when he stepped out of the Outfit plane just before I boarded it to begin my journey to Somalia.

Taking in his deeply tanned face and silver hair, I tried not to let my anger show but could see from his eyes that I'd failed. Rage mounted within me faster than I could stop it. I knew him well, though not as Alan.

To me, this man's name was Cancer.

My mind spewed a fleeting series of memories—being chained in the bar basement during my Outfit selection, Cancer methodically lighting cigarettes and extinguishing them on my bicep, then between my ribs, then bringing a blazing ember to my eyeball.

Viggs had been present for that little soiree, but Cancer had literally scarred me. Those marks became part of my permanent file, a fact confirmed when I overheard the biometrics team examining my body double when Sage faked my death. I heard their words again now as I sat motionless, eyes locked with Cancer.

Raised circular scarring on left bicep and between two left ribs, likely cigarette burns.

Consistent with injuries sustained by subject during Outfit Selection Round 2-2009.

"Hey again, David," he offered, reaching out to shake my hand. "I'm Alan."

His voice had the same Jersey slant that I remembered. So that much hadn't been an act, I thought.

His open palm remained suspended in the space between us. If I didn't accept his handshake, we were done before we began—us as a team, and me as a leader.

Allowing myself a grin, I rose and slapped his hand into my grip a little harder than I intended. Then I pumped his hand into a shake, also a little harder than necessary.

"Fuck that," I said. "Your name may be Alan, but as long as you're on this team, you're going by Cancer."

4

Our helicopter thundered high over the southern edges of Foz do Iguaçu.

A few clouds drifted lazily overhead, but for the most part the sky was clear as we hammered toward the falls like a normal tourist charter. Our pilots flew alongside a murky green swath of the Iguazu River slicing southward through the jungle, a single boat dragging a cresting white wake behind it.

In addition to our five-man team, a single crew chief occupied a drop seat behind one of the pilots. Sergio was beside him, seated atop the coil of thick green rope rising to a metal bracket mounted to the helicopter roof.

Viggs was seated beside me, and I looked toward the other side of the aircraft to see Cancer and Reilly gazing out the window. Beyond them I could make out the eastern curve of the Iguazu River arcing toward a sharp bend. The earth below formed a narrow spike of Brazilian territory pointing southward toward the heart of Argentina. Soon the bend in the river was visible to our front—a mottled convergence of pooling water just below the horizon, with a few streaky white waterfalls spotting the periphery.

The scene inside the helicopter was almost comical, I thought. Sure, we were throttling toward the falls just like any other aircraft filled with gawking tourists. But in our bird, everyone but the pilots and crew chief was dressed like an Army Navy surplus store with legs. Our faces were smeared black and green with camouflage, and our vests bulged with rifle magazines, grenades, fighting knives, and sheathed machetes. Rifles were slung tight to our side next to enormous rucksacks, each an anvil of supplies and explosives for living and fighting in the jungle.

As we neared the spike of river jutting into Argentina, the pilot banked a turn to the right. Beneath us, the gleaming water converged into countless crashing white waterfalls that plunged hundreds of feet across tiered levels of rock forming a single jagged hole toward the center of the earth. From that giant pit rose steaming plumes of mist that floated upward over the jungle.

The Iguazu Falls were a sight of astounding depth and beauty—or at least they would have been, had I the ability to appreciate them. Instead the view elicited a strange thought in me. Parvaneh had offered me a way out of the violent life I'd chosen—indeed, she'd offered me happiness itself, salvation from the darkness. Ironically, however, by the time I'd received her offer, I was inextricably off to war again on a plan of my own devising.

Our helicopter nosed left in a southward turn back toward the falls, following the figure eight pattern of a tourist flight path. Now the majestic view was visible from a closer distance, the sheer magnitude of the scene almost difficult to comprehend. Endless waterfalls formed a wall of ivory flowing across tiers of sheer copper rock face whose horizontal surfaces exploded with trees. Beneath the falls, a churning whitewater procession crawled over giant rocks.

Our helicopter carved back northward to our departure airfield, tracing the Iguazu River's eastern length. And racing low over its shining surface was a tiny white speck—a helicopter identical to ours that had launched from parts unknown and would replace our bird at the departure airfield. The helicopter swap was fast approaching, and I began to steady myself in anticipation.

Before I had time to fully brace for the upcoming maneuver, the pilot cranked a hard clockwise turn down toward the river. My stomach lurched upward as we screamed toward the water's surface while the other helicopter did the opposite and banked up in a sharp corkscrew at maximum throttle. The two birds converged halfway through the mirror-image maneuvers, passing so close that for a pounding moment of terror I was certain we'd have a mid-air collision.

But the other helo roared harmlessly past, and the view beyond our cockpit turned to the Iguazu River's surface as we transitioned to level flight thirty feet above the water before pulling up just over the treetops of the far shore.

"*Phaseline Gold*," the pilot transmitted over my headset. We had just crossed into Argentinian airspace.

"Copy," I replied absently. I glanced at the other men in the aircraft. By virtue of Sergio and Viggs's presence on the team, I had suspected I was being set up for failure. Then, with the appearance of Cancer, I was certain of it. My thoughts fluttered to the same flame that had been attracting them since I spoke to Ian: the coded message.

Had Ian known who my teammates would be? It was

certainly possible, especially since he'd known I was headed for the Triple Frontier in the first place. I looked outside, as if the scenery held some answer or cue from the universe, but saw only verdant, sun-splotched trees sweeping beneath us as the helicopter raced forward.

Now there were no buildings; indeed, no visible civilization of any kind. Instead the earth was impossibly lush, an endless array of treetops untouched by any obstacle, natural or man-made. No wonder they needed a ground team to recon this target, I thought. The emerald treetops hid any semblance of earth from overhead view.

And as the ocean's surface concealed a cosmos of ever-moving sharks, I wondered what monsters roamed beneath the jungle canopy.

The pilot's voice sounded over my headset. "*Rope out at Papa in two mikes.*"

His words brought with them a sudden, looming sense of imminent death. Not in the distant future, but minutes away. The call sign Tomcat couldn't be a coincidence—could it? Did I sense that our infiltration point had been compromised and surrounded already? Was my fear just the result of nerves from being a first-time team leader?

I couldn't tell if I was being paranoid or not, but I knew one thing for certain: I had never been ill-served by following my instincts. They'd been all I had to rely on in the past year since my team had been killed and I'd set out to assassinate the Handler. Ian knew as much about my instincts, and had told me so in our meeting: *If you could blow off a mission abort and still come out of Saamir's building alive, you can make it back from South America.*

"Viper," I transmitted to the pilot, "ground force commander calls diversion from rope point Papa to rope point Echo. I say again, divert to Echo now."

I couldn't call off the mission, but I could divert us from the primary infiltration point to an emergency one—the least likely of four possibilities and, therefore, the least likely to have enemies in the event our plan had been compromised.

A momentary pause.

"Be advised, we haven't received any mission updates from HQ."

"Copy. Now divert to Echo."

"Why the change?"

"Because I'm authorizing it. Ground force commander initials Delta Romeo. Call it in."

"Copy GFC diversion to Echo. Rope out, five mikes."

Sergio looked to me, raising an upward palm for explanation as he saw the helicopter's flight path shift west.

I tucked the mouthpiece under my chin and shouted over the rotor noise, "ROPE POINT ECHO. ROPE POINT ECHO." I held up a hand with fingers spread. "FIVE MINUTES."

The men relayed this change via muffled shouts amid the cabin. Viggs looked irritated—as our point man, he had to adjust to the new route more than any of us.

Sergio squinted at me and pointed at the cockpit. "Pilot call?"

I hooked a thumb toward my chest. "My call."

"What happened?"

I shook my head to indicate it had been a personal decision and saw the disapproval on Sergio's face. Rope point Echo would add nearly a full kilometer to our foot movement—an insignificant distance across open ground, but in the terrain we were about to enter, it could cost us a half-day or worse.

Trying to appear fully convinced of my decision, I

pretended not to notice the expressions of my team. Instead I was recalling the testimony of Watts, the Handler's Chief Vicar of Defense. He'd adamantly opposed my service in any form of leadership capacity. Every word of his testimony was stark in my memory.

Now as for my thoughts on this kid commanding a team in South America? Not a chance. David hasn't got the experience, and frankly, he's not built for that kind of responsibility.

The pilot gave the new two-minute call, which I relayed to the others. There was still nothing to see below but trees. As I gazed at the endless jungle, Watts's final condemnation played out in my mind.

I've read his psychological evaluation, and he's not even in control of his own mind. You put him in charge of Outfit shooters, he's going to get our people killed.

Then the pilot's voice crackled over my headset, mercifully snapping me out of my reverie.

"Thirty seconds."

I held up my index finger and thumb in a C-shape as Sergio echoed the time hack. The crew chief pulled open the sliding door on my side of the aircraft, and warm air whipped inside with a roar. Sightseeing was over— I ripped off my headset and stuffed it beside the pilot's seat, then detached my safety lanyard from its anchor point and hooked it to my kit.

Clear goggles were slung around my neck, and I pulled them over my eyes. Then I unclipped two thick white leather gloves from my gear, sliding them on over my hands as everyone else did the same. Against our camouflage, the oversized white gloves looked ridiculous. Dexterity was nonexistent, shooting a weapon with them inconceivable. They served one purpose only—to absorb the heat and friction of whizzing down a fast rope.

After all, the rope was a tightly braided conglomeration of fiber—not exactly a slick metal fire pole, though the process to descend each was similar. But fast-roping meant the additional weight of weapon, equipment, and ruck—and negotiating the vertical distance as quickly as possible. From rope out to the last man hitting the jungle floor, the helicopter was a stationary target, broadcasting its rotor noise for anyone close enough to hear.

Our helo plunged toward a small opening in the tree-tops. I watched the crew chief rotate the three-foot-long metal bracket out of the aircraft, locking it in place perpendicular to the direction of flight. At the end of the bracket, secured by a locking clasp, was the looped end of our hunter green fast rope.

Sergio positioned himself away from the coiled rope and beside the crew chief. Both were now leaning out the door beside the bracket, looking down—Sergio watching our hole in the treetops and calling adjustments to the crew chief.

"TWENTY FEET!" Sergio yelled. The crew chief keyed his radio, speaking through his mouthpiece to the pilots. Viggs and I struggled to our knees beside the massive coil of green rope, awaiting Sergio's command.

"TEN FEET!"

I looked sideways, seeing Cancer and Reilly adjusting the weight of their rucks as they awaited their turn on the rope.

"FIVE FEET!"

The helicopter lurched to a wobbling hover, treetops whipping in protest below our skids.

"ROPE, ROPE, ROPE!"

Viggs and I pushed the coiled mass of rope off the side of the helicopter. The weighted end spiraled downward in a flash, descending through the rotor wash to disappear into the gap between treetops.

Sergio had only a moment to determine if the rope connected with the ground. If it had become entangled in the trees or fell short of the forest floor, he'd be ordering his men into injury or death.

But he swung his face to Viggs and yelled, "GO!"

Viggs grabbed the rope, swung his legs out of the helo, and vanished over the side.

Then Sergio's eyes met mine.

"GO!"

I reached to the top of the rope, wrapping both hands around its wide girth just below the knot. Sliding my legs over the edge, I pinched the rope between my boots and spun sideways into the void.

My body spiraled clear of the aircraft amid a whipping vortex of tropical air and engine exhaust. Gravity took hold and I dropped like a stone. Tightening the grip of my hands and feet against the rope, I tried to slow the descent.

The view was of a crystalline blue sky being swallowed whole by lurid green jungle. I whipped downward past treetops, trying to catch sight of the ground. But after a flight through blazing sunshine, the space below me looked like a dark pool of shadow.

Glimpses of tree limbs, whipping leaves, tangled vines —then cylindrical tree trunks spun around me. I looked down, my only indication of ground a flash of the rope flaring to its resting place ten feet below. I squeezed my grip as hard as I could, spreading my legs off the rope in a final blazing plunge.

My boots hit hard against soft forest floor. Both knees pulsed with the throbbing pain of impact and I released the rope. Turning away from it before the next man crushed me, I darted a few paces into brush as I grabbed for my rifle. The dull *whomp* of Cancer making landfall sounded as I dropped to a knee. Shifting my rucksack with a twist of my shoulders, I brought my rifle to the ready and bit the fingers of my right work glove to rip it off my hand.

Another *whomp* of a man hitting the ground.

I spat out the glove and felt the grip of my rifle, then scanned for targets to my front. But my eyes were struggling to adjust to the relative darkness, shadows of the infinitely complex jungle layers spreading in every direction.

A final impact sounded as the last man landed, and then the churning noise of helicopter rotors receded.

The aircraft's departure was heralded by the zinging *hiss* of our fast rope falling free, detached by the crew chief. A whipping *thump* of impact erupted as it crashed to the ground, and then we were alone—the helicopter gone, retreating amid the silent depths of jungle all around us.

And what depths they were. An endless expanse of thickly gnarled vines and trees spread before me, plant life thriving in every direction. My stomach churned. It was impossible to see much beyond the dense tree trunks and bushes ringing the tiny clearing. Our touchdown point could be completely surrounded and we'd have not the slightest indication until it was too late. To the enemy, we'd be a real prize: a fully outfitted ground team that just appeared from places unknown, packing millions in equipment and hopefully survivors to be interrogated.

I waited, watching the murky hues of sunlight descend through the leaves above my head, and struggled to control the sound of my quickened breathing in air so hot it felt like we'd fast-roped into a sauna. The thin buzzing of gnats cut through the constant ringing in my ears. I swatted them away, listening alongside the others for any sounds of men or pursuit.

The jungle came to life moments later. First a few tentative birdcalls, then a screeching wail from sources unknown, and then a symphony of uncountable insect species exploding into song.

No gunfire, though, and that was a good start. I looked backward to see Reilly and Cancer running to the rope, hauling its length into a central pile as best they could.

Snatching my loose glove off the ground, I moved to them.

We tossed our goggles and work gloves atop the rope —they served no further use in the jungle. Then Sergio unslung a bulging satchel he'd worn atop his ruck, upending it to dump the contents onto the pile.

Another twenty sets of goggles and gloves tumbled out in a heap atop the rope. This was Sergio's idea, a stroke of genius as far as military deception was concerned. If an enemy patrol stumbled upon our hidden rope, they'd immediately count goggles to determine how many men had infiltrated their territory.

Five invaders might be pursued and dealt with by a local cartel or Hezbollah element. Twenty-five invaders meant a massive incursion, one far more likely to result in multiple enemy radio communications reporting the breach. That meant exponentially higher odds of the Handler's intelligence apparatus overhearing one of these transmissions, and us receiving advance notice that our infiltration was compromised.

Cancer and Reilly piled leaf litter on top of the rope and equipment, a halfhearted attempt at concealment that represented the best we could do under the circumstances.

Viggs pulled up a sleeve to check the GPS on his wrist as he whispered, "Why'd we swap to Echo?"

Sergio answered, "Because the team leader said so. Problem?"

"'Course not, Serge." He made a final adjustment to his GPS, glancing up at me for a second's pause.

Viggs led the way into the jungle with his rifle at the ready. Cancer followed a few steps behind him. I was next, taking my place in the center of our file. Reilly followed behind me. Sergio brought up the rear; as last man in the order of movement, he obscured our back trail by resetting foliage to its original location after he passed.

We moved out quickly, heading a hundred meters due east to distance ourselves from the rope cache. Then we made a ninety-degree dogleg in our route, proceeding another twenty meters before Viggs made an abrupt stop, taking a knee with his rifle pointed forward. The rest of us fell into a tight circle behind him, forming a hasty 360-degree perimeter. There we listened for any indication of pursuit, but heard nothing out of the ordinary. We were infil complete; the mission was on.

Viggs led us in the long march toward our objective.

The jungle around us began to take form as we passed into an area of treetops that allowed more light through and the terrain shifted from shadowy depths to brilliant splendor.

Every conceivable shade of green burst forth in resplendent vividness around us. The jungle appeared so lush and beautiful it seemed like dinosaurs could emerge at any second, as if we'd somehow tread past a threshold long before the existence of man. Two enormous blue butterflies streaked past my head, chasing each other in a fluttering dogfight as I scanned the forest for movement. Everything was so peaceful that it felt like we were on a nature walk, and though that set my nerves at ease, it made me all the more suspicious because things were *never* this easy.

My eye caught movement in the trees to my front left, and my instincts alerted me to danger before my mind registered what I was seeing. The rustle of leaves was too loud, too deliberate for an unscripted breeze. My rifle stock was on my shoulder, the top of my optic meeting the lower edge of my vision as I prepared to engage an unknown enemy.

A fraction of a second later, a definitive form took shape through the leaves just above eye level. I took aim with my optic just as I positively identified it as a cinnamon-colored monkey swinging to a halt on its latest perch as its long tail curled beneath it. The monkey immediately took flight again, leaping to another branch as a second one bounded after it through the trees.

Lowering my rifle, I heaved a sigh and started to glance around to see if anyone had noticed my overreaction.

But a hand was already upon my shoulder as Reilly whispered beside me, "If those monkeys had assault rifles, you'd be dead right now."

We continued patrolling through the sweltering jungle for two hours of slow, deliberate movement. During that time there was constant noise: if not bird and insect calls, then the warbling of a stream that became a call of its own. Once we passed the water, the noise faded to the birds and bugs once more. The harmonics of the jungle were nonstop, varying only in type and intensity.

Sergio had been right about the variable terrain. One

minute the trees were far enough apart that we could've moved at a run if we needed to; the next, we were hacking our way through with machetes.

The sound and scenery provided distraction for a time, but couldn't absolve the strain of walking with a heavy rucksack. I felt like an overburdened snail carrying my house, food, and shelter on my back—a familiar sentiment from my days as a Ranger. Also familiar was the increasing pain in my shoulders, quads, and glutes from humping this weight across the land, exacerbated by my previous bruises. My hip flexors were screaming at me for the two Claymores, five grenades, the double combat load of ammo. Radio batteries were the worst of all—given the overhead cover, how many chances would we have to establish satellite communications?

No sooner had this thought crossed my mind than we saw a glimpse of open sky ahead. By then the faint traces of blue looked almost alien in the sea of mottled green through which we'd been traveling since racing away from the rope point, threading our way through trees and periodic swarms of insects that seemed to rise at random.

Viggs halted the formation, and we set up a local security perimeter. Since our headquarters didn't have FM radio relay in the jungle, we'd be reliant on open patches of sky to make radio shots via satellite antenna.

"You've got to check in," Sergio whispered. "We might not get another chance to report before sunset."

I withdrew my handheld satellite antenna, expanding it into a spindly array of telescoping black spikes.

Then Viggs and I crept to the edge of the clearing, and I aimed the antenna skyward at our preordained azimuth.

Viggs pressed a few buttons on my radio and then whispered, "You're pinging one hundred percent. Should be crystal clear."

"Halo One," I transmitted into my mic, "this is Tomcat Actual."

"Tomcat Actual, this is Halo One. Send your traffic."

"Tomcat is infil complete at Echo. Green on men, weapons, and equipment, how copy?"

"Copy all. State your current location."

For a moment I contemplated sending a grid offset a few hundred meters from our current location. If my instincts were right about our primary infiltration point being compromised, then who could I really trust?

But Viggs would catch this, and I'd already pushed my luck with a last-minute diversion to a different rope point for no justifiable reason. I couldn't risk the guys losing confidence in me or, worse yet, fearing that I was a coward.

So I checked my GPS and sent the accurate ten-digit grid to our location. Wiping a stream of sweat off my eyebrow, I continued, "How copy?"

"Halo One copies all. No operational updates. Continue mission, how copy?"

"Tomcat copies all. Continuing mission."

"Halo One, out."

Viggs and I withdrew from the edge of the clearing and rejoined the others. As we continued moving, I wondered if I'd be punished for sending the correct grid location to headquarters, or if my worst fears were in any way justified.

I received my answer thirty minutes later.

As we patrolled, I listened to the symphony of wildlife around us, shattered by the periodic chirping whistles of some aggressive bird species. If the animals were happy, so was I—silence here meant death, the wildlife going quiet for no predator but man.

Then a new sound caught my ear, one more fearsome

than anything else I could have heard—worse even than silence. At first I prayed my ears were deceiving me, that the distant low tones were something as simple as the snarling of a jaguar. A jaguar wouldn't mess with us, and if it did, we had suppressed weapons to deal with it.

But this sound offered no consolation, making our collective blood run cold at once: the barking of dogs behind us.

We executed evasive maneuvers to throw off their scent, changing direction and moving a couple hundred meters before altering our course again. We proceeded down streams, making landfall only to move off in a new direction. But not only did the barking persist, it also continued to follow us along every sudden change of route. I briefly contemplated whether the enemy on our recon objective would realize they'd been located after the sound of explosions and gunfire a few kilometers away, but based on the mission brief, that kind of activity wasn't uncommon in this region.

The dogs grew closer. We had to lose them—for good.

Finally we hurried into a relatively open, shallow area bordered by steeper high ground to the right. This divot of earth held minimal trees and sparse ground vegetation—I envisioned a Claymore mine exploding from the ridge to our right, my mind's eye projecting the seven hundred steel balls slicing our team into a mangled pile of human bodies.

This was my kill zone.

As we reached the stream at the end of the open patch, I stopped the formation and whispered to Sergio, "Ambush."

"We can't risk our safety—"

"Not ours. Mine. Take the team to that hill ahead. I'll buttonhook here, set an ambush on this side of the stream. Let the bad guys follow my scent instead of the team's."

Pulling the radio and night vision device from my kit, I tossed them to Cancer.

Sergio protested, "You can't set a one-man ambush."

But I'd already dropped my ruck, stripping out a Claymore bandoleer and slinging it over my shoulder.

"Just let me take out the tracking element. Couple of dogs and a tracker or two at most. If I don't meet you in the next twenty minutes, continue mission."

I moved out before he could object further, button-hooking toward my ambush area while Sergio led Viggs, Cancer, and Reilly across the stream.

Now I had everything I needed to complete a one-man ambush, and nothing more. If I was killed, the team could split up everything of value from my ruck and continue mission.

I located a vantage point that allowed me to peer twenty meters into the low center of my kill zone—I'd initiate the ambush from here. Reaching into the Claymore bandoleer, I pulled the spool of brown wire and hastily tied one end around the narrow base of a bush. Then I unspooled the rest of the wire toward the edge of the high ground.

The Claymore mine was a staple of any defensive position or ambush, and emplacing one was a basic infantry task. Setting up a Claymore was like riding a bike; doing so under the current circumstances, however, was more like riding a bike amid a bloodthirsty pack of wolves. And the bike would explode if you pedaled wrong.

I could plainly hear the dogs gaining ground as I reached the edge of the rise, the depression before me spread out in a perfect kill zone—provided I didn't screw anything up. A tree at the edge would serve as my protection from the mine's back blast.

The Claymore itself was innocuous enough in appearance: a slightly curved, olive-drab plastic rectangle with metal stakes that I planted into the earth. If it wasn't for the presence of the words FRONT TOWARD ENEMY on the convex side, you could practically mistake it for a piece of gardening equipment.

After angling the front of the mine downward into the kill zone, I tied the opposite side of brown wire around the sprouting offshoot of a young tree. Then I unscrewed a plastic L-shaped plug from the top of the mine and carefully pulled the very end of the brown wire from its resting place inside the spool.

The wire ended in a cylindrical, silver blasting cap that I avoided touching, instead threading its wire through a slit in the shipping plug and pulling taut. Inserting the blasting cap into the top of the mine, I screwed the L-shaped plug back in before giving a final adjustment to the mine's fatal orientation.

Piling a handful of leaf litter before the Claymore served as the only camouflaging effort I'd have time for—besides, by the time my pursuing enemies could make out the green plastic in the forest, I'd be clacking it off in their faces.

Hearing the rustle of brush to my left, I felt a shock of horror that I was too late—if the pursuit team burst into the clearing now, I'd be outmatched in a battle of one rifle against many.

But instead, I saw not enemy fighters but a mangy, hideous dog gleefully bounding forward along my back trail. I quietly edged myself backward, seeing a second dog follow in the first's trail. This one looked like a German Shepherd on steroids, and smelling wasn't on his agenda—he simply trotted behind the first dog, his ears up.

I felt the sinking realization that one dog was released to follow my smell, and the second to eat whatever human waited at the end of the scent trail. They passed out of sight, moving toward my buttonhook maneuver at the stream.

Easing myself backward, I began to catch sight of a single human figure crashing through the brush after the dogs—doubtless the tracker, followed in short order by the enemy fighters.

I crouched low, racing back along the length of Claymore wire to my original tie-down point. There I recovered the firing device, a boxlike assembly with a clickable handle on one side that I feverishly plugged the brown wire into before flicking the safety off. My next glance into the kill zone revealed a single man passing through at a run, following his hounds with a rifle slung on his back. A tracker, not a fighter, I thought, though I wouldn't be so lucky with whoever he led toward me.

The lead dog was braying now, a whooping howl that grew louder as he approached me along a progressively fresher trail. His noise mercifully allowed me to track his progress along the arcing buttonhook. Arranging my rifle at my side and cupping the mine's firing device with both hands, I prepared for two near-simultaneous actions: clacking off the Claymore as the fighters passed through my kill zone, then readying my rifle to shoot the dogs off my back before the second one ripped the face from my skull.

My pursuers gradually became visible at the far edge of the kill zone, still too far for me to target with the Claymore.

I was too low to see much of them other than a

glimpse of four men with automatic weapons carried at the ready. They were moving in a hasty tactical wedge, looking seasoned and confident. Four men weren't enough to commit against a recon team, and this had only one explanation: they weren't an independent team but scouts for a larger element. They didn't need to wipe us out, only locate us, report our position, and initiate the cat-and-mouse maneuvering between us and something far more deadly.

My blood began to curl as the lead dog's howling grew louder much sooner than I hoped.

The four men proceeded into my kill zone, looking confused—why was this stupid dog running back toward them from the side? The proximity made it inconceivable that a single man lay in hiding in between. Their continued forward movement assured me they had assumed the dog had made a mistake.

Now I heard the dog braying from directly behind me —he was closing the final stretch, and soon the crashing of brush to my rear outpaced the barks.

The second dog had seen me and was charging ahead for the kill.

I had time for a final fleeting assessment of the four pursuers—they were still moving, just beginning to enter my kill zone but far from centered in front of my Claymore. Glancing over my shoulder, I saw the charging black animal rushing toward me.

Dropping the firing device, I grabbed my rifle and rolled onto my back. I'd only managed to angle my rifle suppressor toward a flash of white jaws amid the dark, hairy mass before I began shooting as quickly as I could pull the trigger.

With a final yelp, the black shape crashed to the ground and slid to a halt against my boots.

Automatic gunfire pelted the earth around me a moment later, four weapons chattering from the kill zone. Trying to stay low, I rolled to my stomach and fumbled for the mine's firing device. Clawing the boxlike chunk of plastic within my grip, I blindly began pressing the handle downward as dirt rained down on me from adjacent bullet impacts.

Twice the firing device gave a flat tactile *clack* of impotence before the third attempt fired the Claymore.

The deafening explosion ceased all sound of incoming gunfire, filling the forest with a low, reverberating boom like the crack of thunder. Leaf litter, soil, and tree bark blew over me with gale force. I waited until the debris finished clattering down before blinking my eyes open to assess the kill zone as I brought my rifle into a prone firing position.

It was impossible to see anything—the depression was hidden beyond a billowing mass of gray smoke, though I could hear the groaning wails of at least two men. No orders being shouted, no one coming to their aid much less continuing to shoot at me.

Setting down my rifle, I lobbed two grenades into the din.

Their twin explosions silenced the screams, though as the echo faded I began to hear movement—not to my front, but rather my flank. I aimed toward the noise, gradually discerning that it was moving away: the tracker, trying to escape.

I leapt to my feet and sprang after him, frantic to erase any survivors who could assist another pursuit. But first I caught sight of the lead dog, the one who'd followed my scent.

The shaggy animal was setting a land speed record in an attempt to follow the sound of the tracker. Stopping to raise my rifle, I took careful aim and picked off the hound with two shots that sent him somersaulting to a stop.

I took off again, easily following the sound of a man moving clumsily through the brush before catching sight of him.

He was careening through the jungle in a full panic, his body grazing trees as he stumbled forward.

Then he tripped and fell before scrambling to his feet and plunging forward into the brush once more.

"HEY!" I yelled after him.

He turned, raising his hands shakily, panic in his eyes. His rifle was an old Enfield still slung askew on his back, and I heard and smelled him evacuate his bladder and bowels at the sight of me. I fired twice into his gut, followed by a single round to his head.

The action was as reflexive as a fistfight, two jabs and a hook, and the man fell forward into a fetal position.

Racing past his body to the stream, I crossed it and began moving uphill.

* * *

I moved up the high ground as quickly as I could, sacrificing every trace of stealth for speed. What choice did I have? If I lost contact with my team, I became an evader without provisions or a radio. Given the enemy force I'd just encountered, it didn't take an honors math major to realize my odds of survival on my own were zilch.

So I frantically sped along, pulling myself upward using tree trunks when the ground became too steep, leaving reckless smears of boot prints in the earth as I scrambled for purchase. I was moving in the team's general direction, hoping they'd hear me breaking brush toward them.

But no one came, and I began to panic. It was the opposite of claustrophobia—I was in too large a space, too vast a wilderness to conceivably negotiate it alone. My mind began to layer in horrid possibilities like a checklist of terror. The team thought reinforcing enemies had caused me to run in the opposite direction. They assumed I stood no chance in the first place, and abandoned me the second I struck out alone in order to increase their distance—and thus their chances of continuing the mission. No, they'd never abandon a man alive; instead, they'd heard me dispatch the tracker and assumed the final gunshots indicated my own execution.

I heard a rustle and froze. Then I detected movement to my right and spun to orient my rifle.

An animal burst through the foliage toward me, its movements almost doglike, its pink tongue flickering forward through the brush. Another second's observation revealed it to be a lizard, with dark stripes weaving an ornate pattern of scales across its stout body. The reptile stopped abruptly at the sight of me, flicking its tongue in my direction before turning and clambering unhurriedly over a fallen branch and sliding back into the undergrowth.

I'd just continued moving when I heard a voice whisper, "Boss."

I stopped in place, searching for the source as I lowered my weapon. Then I heard the brush move beside me a moment before Viggs appeared. His eyes darted over my body, checking for wounds, before he said, "Follow me."

I chased his figure along the hillside as he raced forward, guiding me toward a dense jungle grove where Sergio, Cancer, and Reilly were pulling security outward.

Sergio's expression was inscrutable as he said, "Suit up."

Seeing my rucksack in the center of their formation, I threw it on my back and adjusted the straps.

Reilly's head was shaking in reverence. "That was pretty heavy shit you did there, sir."

"David," I corrected him.

"David. Sir. Boss. Whatever—that was heavy."

Cancer interceded, handing me my radio and night vision device. I replaced them in my pouches as he said, "Fuck that. Your name may be David"—he gave a jagged grin—"but as long as you're on this team, you're going by Suicide."

My mind jolted at this, recalling my old team referring to me by the same name and the Handler parroting the reference in my job interview for the Somalia mission. Then I thought about Ian's words, how he kept assuring me that if I could kill Saamir and escape, I could also return from South America alive.

Why would he say that? He knew I'd already been to war. I'd fought men in combat in Afghanistan, Iraq, the US, Somalia, Brazil, and Myanmar. Through it all, my perpetual death wish had overshadowed any fear of dying.

Why was he trying to console me about returning alive?

An explanation began forming in my mind. It wasn't the meaning of Ian's message, just an implication. But within seconds, I couldn't refute it.

Cancer was now grinning widely while Reilly suppressed a quiet chuckle. Viggs put a hand on my shoulder and gave me a shake, waking me from my reverie.

"That's it." He nodded. "Best Outfit call sign since you

changed Alan's name to Cancer. Welcome to the war, Suicide."

Sergio was glancing back at me, saying nothing, but his eyes conveyed that we needed to leave—a fact I needed no reminding about.

I pushed myself up to a knee, gripping my M4.

My mind was scrambled between the fading rush of combat action and the references to my first team— Cancer crowning me Suicide, Viggs and Reilly calling me Boss—and I recalled what Boss himself had told me before his final mission, a premonition that I'd be giving orders one day. The swirling mess was underscored by an even greater concern, a fact I was beginning to inherently know as surely as I stood in the jungle of Argentina.

The Handler was trying to have us wiped out.

Not just me but my entire team, down to a man, and for the second time in recent memory. His first attempt had been successful, and I'd lost Boss, Matz, Ophie, and Karma as a result. Only I could ensure he didn't succeed again, and this time, I wouldn't fail those around me.

"All right, guys." I nodded to Sergio. "Suicide says it's time to go. Viggs, lead us out."

* * *

We moved until night began to fall beneath the canopy, finding no break in the overhead cover that we could exploit to make radio contact with the satellite. The jungle roof hastened darkness, and we made our way into the densest brush we could find to bed down for the night. Viggs took a ninety-degree turn from our direction of movement, threading his way into a black cluster of trees.

At this deep heart of the jungle, the densest a rain-forest could be while remaining passable to humans, the humidity swelled to choking levels of panic. I pulled at my shirt collar, trying to expose my sweat-soaked skin to air but finding none. The vegetation was so thick here that air circulation was impossible; nothing could enter but water from above, and once in this microcosm of wet jungle floor and black shadows, it couldn't leave either. A flock of mosquitos formed a tangled knot of movement around my face. One swat knocked ten out of the way only to make room for another ten. The effect was maddening.

Sergio whispered, "We need to rest here."

"Rest?" I replied. "We can't *breathe* here."

"That's why it's perfect." He swiped a cloud of mosquitos from his face and jerked a thumb over his shoulder. "Claymore covering our backside where we turned off the trail. We sleep back-to-back, shoulder-to-shoulder with two men awake at all times. One of them holds the firing device."

He must have seen worry in my face, because he went on, "Our objective isn't compromised just because you blasted a Claymore back there. Don't worry, we'll continue mission."

But he misinterpreted my concern. I wasn't worried about compromise. I didn't think we were intended to reach that objective alive, and if we did show up on site, we weren't going to make it out.

I nodded to Sergio. "All right. Let's get set up."

Cancer and Viggs pulled security while Reilly prepared a Claymore mine for our defense. I watched Sergio, considering whether to tell him about my suspicions. If I wanted to speak to Sergio alone, it was now or never. Would he dismiss me as a lunatic or worse? Probably. He'd seen my Outfit psychological evaluation. So had Parvaneh's bodyguard, and his testimony on my current assignment had been as damning as possible.

He's been formally diagnosed with depression, suicidal ideation, posttraumatic stress, and alcoholism. If he's going to be employed at the Outfit, it should be in a highly supervised capacity, not in a position of leadership that he's neither earned nor demonstrated any aptitude for.

By measure of loyalty to the Organization, Sergio was the last person I should speak to about my suspicions. But he was my second-in-command, and it was up to both of us to confide in one another and determine the best way forward.

I touched Sergio's arm and nodded away from the others. He followed me a short distance and we crouched next to each other. I glanced toward the men to ensure they weren't close enough to hear before whispering, "I think the Handler's trying to kill us."

"That's bullshit," he said flatly. "It's outright treasonous, David. The Outfit doesn't hunt their own unless someone goes rogue. And this team isn't going rogue on my shift."

"I didn't say the Outfit was trying to kill us. I said the Handler."

"If that were true, there'd be no 'trying' about it. We'd be dead."

I thought about the Handler's elaborate deception in the garden when Parvaneh and I returned from Rio. He'd allowed me to smuggle a weapon toward him just so I'd be killed in the ensuing assassination attempt, an elaborate ploy meant only to deceive his daughter. But I couldn't tell those particulars to Sergio, a fanatical loyalist who must never learn that I'd joined the Outfit solely to kill the Handler.

"Sergio, I've met the Handler and seen his methods. He'd make our deaths look like a combat loss. And if we hadn't diverted from our primary infiltration point, I think that would have happened already."

Sergio was scanning for the others, making sure we weren't overheard. "You sound insane. You mustn't let the others hear you speaking like this."

I gave a heavy sigh, wishing I could explain what had happened to Boss's team. But that, too, was something I could never speak of to anyone in the Outfit, much less in Sergio's presence.

Instead, I went for a pragmatic approach. "We walked for hours today without seeing anyone, and thirty minutes after I report our location we're getting hit. The men I killed weren't tracking us with dogs in the middle of the jungle by accident—someone sent them our way."

Sergio grimaced slightly, and I could tell he wasn't convinced. But before he could reply, Viggs approached us and spoke in a hushed voice.

"Security is set, gents. Guys are rotating weapons maintenance and chow."

Sergio looked to me, saying nothing.

I nodded. "Thanks. Let's initiate our rest plan ASAP."

Viggs turned and Sergio rose to follow, then paused for a moment to whisper in my ear.

"I don't want to hear you mention this to anyone else. Understand?"

He didn't wait for a response.

I remained kneeling as he walked away, turning to relieve myself in the bushes before bedding down for the night. But relieving myself was an optimistic term for what occurred. I peed a weak stream of dark, stinking amber fluid that noiselessly vanished into the wet earth. I'd been drinking water as fast as I could since we arrived, supplementing my intake with salt tablets, and I was nonetheless severely dehydrated. We all were. Water resupply wasn't difficult; there were endless sources to use to refill our drinking vessels, and we carried enough iodine tablets to purify drinking water for weeks. But it was simply impossible to drink fast enough to take in a sufficient amount of water to offset the constant oozing of sweat in this place.

I joined the others as we settled into back-to-back position before our surroundings turned to total blackness. We kept our rucks on, night vision atop our heads but turned off to conserve battery, and rifles across our laps.

We were getting decimated by mosquitos.

I whispered to Cancer beside me, "Don't they know we have repellant on?"

"Try the mud," he replied.

Seeing that he was doing the same, I took handfuls of the dark earth and smeared it across my face and neck. We tightened our collars and cuffs and donned gloves, pulling every spare inch of cloth around us. The effect was twofold: first, to keep the mosquitos away, and second, to stay warm.

The temperature was dropping into the sixties—no trouble if dry, but after a day in the forest, our sweat-soaked fatigues clung to us like freezing rags. I would have killed for a campfire, if not for warmth then just to keep the bugs at bay.

Our position put us in constant physical contact, and when I started to shiver first, the movement became almost contagious. Soon our collective mass was shuddering with the relative cold as mosquitos dove in for exposed skin, the narrow zinging hum of their constant movement around us as bad as their bites. I was certain that sleep would elude me that night as it had for many others where I was in a comfortable bed, much less suffocating in the jungle.

But the physical rigors, adrenal outpours, and constant vigilance of a combat patrol did strange things to one's body when they were finally alleviated, however fleetingly. By the time my guard shift arrived, Cancer had to shake me out of a far deeper sleep than I was capable of in the outside world.

PENANCE

Oderint dum metuant

-Let them hate, so long as they fear

5

At the first signs of sunrise, the two men on guard duty nudged their sleeping teammates awake. Consciousness was confirmed when bodies began shivering with the cold, and we all rose to a knee with our rifles at the ready. This was "stand-to," a time-honored tactic of maintaining full security during the first and last periods of daylight. Most American soldiers traced the practice back to when the French and Indians were most likely to attack in the eighteenth century, but it was probably employed long before that. That time of day meant there was enough light to attack during periods when the enemy was likely to be complacent.

To say we broke camp after stand-to would be an overstatement. There was little to do but store our night vision, recover the Claymore mine, and perform a quick map check to verify our route. Then, we continued our march south through the jungle.

The sun's heat penetrated the tangled branches and vines above us, gradually reaching the forest floor and sending great billowing blankets of steam tumbling like smoke through the trees. Foggy rays of sunlight cast a golden glow, the rays deflected by slick leaves and shimmering in a thousand directions. We maintained a good pace through the morning, patrolling undisturbed amid the lilting chorus of insects and frogs. Soon their song was joined by countless birds.

Once we warmed up with the movement of patrolling, I felt better than I had yesterday. A certain hardness and fortitude set in by the second day on the march as you're continually exposed to the elements and further removed from a comfortable bed and regular meals. The combined effect would forge us with an escalating toughness, right up until the point of diminishing returns that we had yet to reach.

The terrain we crossed made for as easy a march as the jungle was capable of, and we took no rest breaks beyond stopping when we came across a stream. We took turns downing all the water we could stomach from our own supply before refilling our vessels from the natural water source. Dropping in iodine tablets, we noted the time and continued moving. Within forty-five minutes, the tablets would purify the groundwater to a sufficiently drinkable, if medicinally flavored, state.

Another hour's march elapsed before Viggs halted the patrol and pointed to a gap in the treetops.

"Should be able to make a comms shot here."

I was skeptical—the gap wasn't large, but it provided a slight view of clear sky along the rough azimuth we'd need to hit the satellite. Viggs suggested setting up an antenna on a tripod to make the shot, so we established local security as he prepared his equipment.

I scanned the surrounding area. To our left flank was a steep drop into a gulley that rose into a hill on the far side.

Cancer was pulling security toward the gulley, and I crouched beside him.

"Hey, Cancer."

"Yes, Suicide?"

I pointed at the hillside across the gorge. "Pop quiz: can you get me a ten-digit grid to that hillside?"

He followed my finger to the patch of open ground across from us. The gulch was only eighty meters away at most, but it represented a significant obstacle, simply too deep and thickly jungled to move through on foot.

"Shit, playa," he answered, retrieving a handheld binocular device from his kit. Holding it steady with both hands, he pressed a button to make a laser shot. Without moving his eyes from the device, he recited the grid reading projected across his magnified view.

I jotted the grid on my waterproof notepad, reading it back to him to be certain. By then Viggs was waving me over—he'd assembled his tripod topped with a satellite antenna and appeared confident about the signal he was getting.

"Thanks," I said to Cancer without explanation, and moved to Viggs.

Viggs whispered, "We're pinging eighty percent from here. Should work."

He handed me the radio handset, and I noticed with irritation that Sergio was kneeling beside me to supervise my transmission.

"Halo One," I said into the handset, "this is Tomcat Actual."

Ten seconds passed, and I attempted the transmission again before hearing a response.

"*Tomcat Actual, this is Halo One. You're coming in broken but readable. Send your traffic.*"

I squinted up at the treetops clustering my narrow view of open sky, unsurprised that my transmission was breaking up—with this much overhead cover, they were lucky to be hearing me at all.

"Tomcat had troops in contact, vicinity our last reported grid, break." I released the transmit button, and then keyed it again. "No friendly casualties. Five enemies killed in action, how copy?"

"Copy all. Send your current location, over."

While I read back the numbers from my waterproof notepad, I saw Sergio checking my report against his own GPS. Noting the discrepancy, he grabbed my sleeve and shook his head. I pulled my arm away.

"Say again current location, over."

Sergio snatched my notepad away and stuffed it in his pocket.

Then, leaning into my ear so Viggs wouldn't hear, he hissed, "Quit fucking around. Give them our location."

I made defiant eye contact with Sergio as I re-transmitted the false grid from memory. Then I added, "Anticipate we'll be in position before nightfall. Over."

"Halo One copies all. Operational update follows, break." Sergio's eyes were fierce—my false report had severely pissed him off. *"Report of enemy patrol passing one klick south along your route, break. Remain in place one hour before Charlie Mike, how copy?"*

I raised my eyebrow to Sergio. He shook his head, unconvinced.

"Tomcat copies all. Will rest in place one hour before continuing mission."

"Halo One, out."

I handed Viggs the handset and he began breaking down the communications equipment.

Predictably, Sergio pulled me away from the others to speak in private.

"What the fuck were you thinking, David?"

I was unapologetic. "If I'm wrong about us being targeted, then reporting a slightly altered grid costs us nothing."

"Do you have any idea what will happen to you if they find out you gave a false report? What will happen to me for allowing it?"

"They're not going to find out. The grid wasn't far off—just on that hillside across the gulley. Now here's my play: while we wait, we're going to hide as best we can and perform a hasty reconnaissance on that hillside."

"Why?"

"Because I bet you a case of beer that it's going to be crawling with enemies before the hour's up."

"You're wrong." He dismissed me and rolled up his cuff to start a timer on his watch. "But you're on."

"Just tell the guys we're using the hour halt as a quick rehearsal."

"Oh, don't worry, David. I will. Because the alternative is to tell them their team leader is paranoid, delusional, and bordering on treason."

* * *

Sergio's final words burned in my mind as time ticked down our one-hour wait. I could feel his anger—hell, there wasn't much I couldn't feel right now, positioned close enough to the others to hear them breathe.

My idea to conduct a rehearsal reconnaissance had been a well-intentioned ploy to safeguard our team against an inbound enemy force while maintaining the status quo of business as usual.

The problem, pointed out to me only after Sergio had disseminated the order, was that no patch of vegetation suitably large enough for stationary reconnaissance existed nearby—and without time to dig a hide site or otherwise prepare extensive camouflage, we'd been restricted to hiding wherever we could.

As it turned out, the densest brush we could find while maintaining eyes on the far hill was almost ludicrously small for a five-man team. Granted, the plant growth was thick enough to make us practically invisible unless someone broke brush and stepped on top of us, but the end result was five men piled nearly back-to-back into a tangle of vines in a rocky divot amid the jungle.

Sergio whispered, "That's one hour. Case of beer, David."

"Who?" Cancer asked.

"Suicide," Sergio played along. "I meant Suicide."

"Ah. Okay."

I whispered back, "Let's give it another thirty minutes."

Sergio shook his head. "We're losing light. We were instructed to wait one hour, so that's what we'll wait."

"Our instructions were to wait *at least* one hour. My discretion says give it another thirty."

He released a measured exhale, surely steeling himself from talking back to me in front of the others.

But Reilly, picking up on the disparity, briefly turned his head to glance at me.

"Lot of jungle between us and our objective, David, and we're supposed to have eyes on by 2300 tonight. Why do you want to keep waiting?"

I struggled to find a plausible excuse, something that would match Sergio's standard of trust in our mission. Maybe he was right—they'd all think I was paranoid. Maybe I *was* paranoid, I thought. I remembered being on the run in Rio, having the same thought and trying to convince Parvaneh and her bodyguard that the

Handler was trying to kill us. I hadn't known then that Parvaneh was his daughter. She dismissed the Handler from suspicion, declaring, *That's the one thing about this situation I can tell you with total certainty*. And she was right.

But that didn't mean Sergio was.

Ultimately I decided to level with them. "I think the Handler's trying to kill us. And make it look like a combat loss."

"David," Sergio said, "I told you—"

Viggs interjected, "Hang on a second, Serge. I gotta hear this for myself. David, I was wondering why you diverted infiltration points yesterday. I never blame a fighting man for trusting his instincts, but I can tell you one thing: we wouldn't need to be a combat loss. When the Handler wants someone dead, they're dead."

"Ordinarily I'd agree with you. But in this case he's got certain...considerations. Because of his daughter."

Reilly asked, "The brunette in Rio?"

"Yeah."

"Nice," he hissed, picking up on the unspoken. He'd seen Parvaneh and me together in the plane and could draw his own conclusions.

Sergio said, "No one's trying to kill us but the enemy. We got spotted making comms yesterday. They pursued. That's it."

I replied, "In the middle of the jungle? I don't think it's that simple."

Then Cancer whispered, "Yesterday's contact might have been too close for coincidence, but I still don't buy Suicide's theory. Viggs, could our call to higher have been intercepted?"

"On the Organization's encrypted network? Not a chance. But even if we didn't get spotted, I don't know why the Handler would be trying to wax us. What else you selling, Suicide?"

I offered, "I like my alternate theory a lot less than blaming the Handler."

"What alternate theory?"

"That we've got a mole in this team."

Sergio fumed, "Where do you get off? You show up here, get us pulled off our teams—"

I vaguely registered the angry cadence of his words as he went on while observing the others' reactions, trying to determine who, if anyone, was having an oh-shit moment.

Sergio was stern and angry as always—I couldn't tell anything there. Reilly looked incredulous and dismissive, while Cancer was watching me strangely, either wondering where I came from or fearing that I'd found out something I shouldn't have. Viggs was completely mission-focused, either innocent or the best actor I'd ever seen.

I felt everyone's gaze upon me as they glanced back from their security positions, then I realized Sergio had stopped whispering.

Cancer seemed to detect that I was unconvinced of my teammates' innocence. "Look here. You think there's a mole? You can put that baby to bed right now. Better yet, smother it with a pillow. Know why, asshole?"

"Why?" I shot back.

"Because a death sentence to one of us is a death sentence to all. We're a five-man team in Indian country. No one's getting the others compromised and living to tell about it, you get me? Now I'm in this racket for the thrills, so you can talk about the Handler all you want. But I ain't gonna tolerate you questioning our team when we're all in this shit together."

I considered his words as my gaze fell to the undergrowth. My rational side insisted that everything in this criminal underworld came with its double crosses—Jais had betrayed Boss's team, Gabriel had betrayed Parvaneh, Sage had betrayed the Handler himself, and I had betrayed Sage.

But instinctively, I knew better.

"You're right, Cancer," I said, closing my eyes. "I'm sorry. I've run into some real bogeymen since going to the Mist Palace, so now I see them everywhere. Even among brothers." Then I opened my eyes, feeling ashamed. "Let's get moving."

"About fucking time." Viggs was the first to stand, his popping knees and the slight rustling of brush around him almost deafening after a stationary hour in the grove. I started to rise as well, but Viggs grabbed my shoulder and violently thrust me back down.

Then Sergio threw a hand over my mouth while using his other hand to hold me in place—a field mutiny? Why not, I thought bitterly. We were playing Vietnam rules in the jungle, with virtually no oversight—they could frag their officer and leave me in the bush. No one outside the team would be any the wiser.

But when I looked up, I saw Viggs had planted his back against the tree behind him, eyes scanning the direction we'd come from. His left hand was formed into a fist. Whatever he'd seen, he'd determined it was too close to risk further movement.

Sergio released me and I followed Viggs's gaze, but I was too low in the underbrush to see anything.

Viggs switched his hand from a fist telling us to cease movement to three outstretched fingers. Index, middle, and ring.

Three enemies visible.

Then he raised a fourth finger, extending his thumb a moment later so his hand was open.

Five enemies.

We remained completely immobile, uncertain of the enemies' distance but certain they were close enough to hear us.

Why couldn't we hear them?

Viggs started ticking off fingers on the opposite hand. Six, seven, eight. Then he cringed, his hands going limp to release their count. He made a single fist now, flashing the hand open and closed three times.

Fifteen.

His hands moved to his rifle, the count complete. With fifteen enemy fighters sighted, that was little consolation. I was freaking out, and quite certain that the others were as well. For all our combined combat experience, we stood little chance against those odds in the best of circumstances, much less with all five of us bundled into a reconnaissance position where a well-placed hand grenade would wipe us out.

I could now hear movement outside of our hiding spot, first the low rustle of men moving through the jungle and then a few quiet voices. Whoever was approaching had decent noise discipline but clearly was not too concerned about being heard.

Of course they weren't. I knew exactly what was happening, saw it unfolding like a roadmap inside my head even before I had any confirmation. In theory, they could have followed our tracks here.

But I knew that wasn't the case.

They were operating off the grid I falsely reported to headquarters. The decision was a good one on my part, enough to save the team—but I hadn't anticipated from which direction the enemy would approach. I'd tried to place the gulley between our actual location and the one I reported, thinking the terrain would allow us to slip away unnoticed.

Instead, the enemy had come from the same direction as us and were seeking the best possible vantage point to watch the opposite hillside: the same spot we now occupied.

I didn't have any verifiable confirmation that the enemy received the false grid I had reported to my own headquarters, but it didn't matter. I got that verification sixty seconds later, when the sound of movement shifted behind me, opposite the gulley, and receded into the distance. A decisive victory for us, if only Viggs had visibly relaxed to indicate the entire enemy force had departed to flank around the gulley and pursue our reported location.

Instead, he remained as alert as ever. He pointed his hand over his shoulder, then flashed four fingers.

Four enemies remained in place—why?

My answer came via an intricate series of hand signals that I could barely follow. Viggs placed his hand in front of his forehead, then extended his index and middle fingers upward like the sign for the number two—two bars on his hat. Rank, a captain? Must have meant an enemy commander.

Then index and thumb pressed against the side of his face, pantomiming a telephone. A radio operator, I thought, confirming his first signal had been the commander.

But he'd indicated four enemies—who were the other two?

Then Viggs touched the tip of his forefinger and thumb together to form a circle, holding it to one eye. Seeing my confusion, he pretended to hold a rifle and squint into a scope.

Two snipers.

Now it all made sense: an overwatch element remained. Commander, his radio operator, and two snipers assuming the best possible vantage point to control their maneuver element as the other fighters—eleven, by Viggs's count—had flanked the gulley to find us.

The ground team was trying to flush us into the snipers' line of fire, and if that failed, they'd sweep through and finish us off.

Despite Viggs's tense expression, I couldn't help myself—I raised my upper body slightly on one elbow to peer past a tree trunk.

Then I lowered myself back down, having seen enough: the shapes of two men kneeling beside each other. A commander and his radio operator, the latter preparing communications and the former speaking into a hand mic, the same as Viggs and I had done during my contact with our Outfit headquarters just over an hour earlier, and likely in the same spot.

We'd escaped death by a hair already, my instincts prevailing without any corresponding sense of relief because we weren't out of the proverbial woods yet: the slightest overt noise, much less an audible gunshot, would result in the maneuver element reversing course to overrun us.

Then I heard men quietly speaking Spanish—a language that only Sergio knew. Looking over, I saw him slowly, deftly pulling my waterproof notepad from his pocket. He must have been preparing to jot a note to me in order to communicate silently.

To my great consternation, though, a writing utensil never appeared in his hand. Instead he listened, appearing focused and, for all intents and purposes, enraptured by the two men speaking in Spanish. Then the dialogue ceased, fusing into one voice murmuring in a tone far too official for conversation.

The commander was transmitting to his headquarters.

Sergio glanced to my notepad as he listened to the lengthy stream of Spanish numerals.

We made brief eye contact, and Sergio nodded gravely. I shot him a cocky wink; the enemy had just recited the exact grid I'd transmitted on the Handler's encrypted satellite network.

The sole advantage we had was in our concealment—we'd capitalized on the less than advantageous terrain by slipping into the densely vegetated divot that virtually concealed us from outside view. Right now, we had one course of action: wait until the ground element cleared the opposite hillside without finding us, leaving the commander no choice but to continue pushing south and try to overrun us along our route to the objective.

I looked back to Sergio, showing him a closed fist and then tapping my wristwatch. *Wait them out.* He nodded back, as if my conclusion was too stupidly obvious to bother communicating. Scowling, I looked away just as we heard approaching footsteps.

The soft shuffling of leaf litter sounded like the movement of an individual. Cancer was watching the opposite side of the trunk, apparently able to see the man advancing. Viggs watched Cancer's face, trying to discern any information he could about who was approaching behind him.

Then, the footsteps stopped abruptly—had he spotted us?

Cancer's face creased into a smile of amused disbelief, and a second later we heard a stream of liquid splashing on the ground.

The enemy was peeing on the other side of Viggs's tree.

I grinned to myself, a brief thought flashing amid the tension and terror: *this will make a great story if we get out of here alive.*

Glancing upward to Viggs, I saw him smiling too.

These men were steel, I thought, undaunted in the face of danger. How was I supposed to be a part of their ranks, much less lead them? I'd asked the Handler for too much in requesting leadership of an Outfit team, over-stepped my capabilities and experience by too wide a margin.

But these men would see me through it—I knew that in my core, and felt a wave of comfort blossoming in me.

Until Viggs's smile faded, along with the sound of urine hitting the tree behind him.

Then more rustling of undergrowth beyond our posi-tion—the enemy had seen or sensed something, and was moving to investigate.

What happened next seemed to transpire over the course of an eternity, but on reflection was likely two seconds, if that.

Viggs reached for his knife, but Cancer shook his head and flashed his hands into two fists. Upon seeing Viggs nod, Cancer slid his own knife from its sheath.

Without warning, Viggs rolled sideways and reached out with both hands, pulling the enemy into our grove with a sharp crash of brush.

The first thing I saw was the man's mouth gaping open and closed like a fish—Viggs had an immense hand clamped around his throat, crushing his larynx at maximum force while holding him immobile with the other forearm braced across his chest.

I pulled my arm away from the trickle of urine that

sprayed my sleeve as Cancer rose to a knee and slid his blade into the man's kidney. The man's mouth opened in rigid stillness, and Viggs maneuvered his prey sideways so Cancer could stick the kidney on the opposite side.

Reilly and Sergio were standing now, audibly rustling the vines around us as they took aim with their suppressed weapons.

The sound of automatic rifle actions clanking forward and back was louder than the shots themselves as subsonic rounds puffed out of the suppressors. I remained still and out of their line of fire, resisting my urge to look despite Sergio and Reilly's continued shooting, which went far beyond what was necessary—I could *hear* bodies falling in the jungle beyond our hiding spot, could sense bullets spearing flesh.

But as they stopped shooting only long enough to reload, I realized they had been taking no chances, that they planned to continue firing until a moan or wail of agony was outside the realm of possibility.

After reloading, they pushed forward out of our hiding spot. At this signal, Viggs dropped the dead man in his grasp like a bag of trash into a landfill. Cancer sheathed his knife, leaping up to follow Viggs into the open.

By the time I'd cleared the dense brush, my team was already rolling the other three bodies, performing a hasty search for anything of intelligence or resupply value. Cancer slapped Sergio's shoulder as the latter searched a body, presumably to relieve the second-in-command so he could turn his faculties to more strategic matters.

Sergio relinquished his kill, then rose and turned to stare at me before advancing quickly, stopping a step before he would've chest-bumped me.

He whispered, "Hey, shithead."

"Yeah?"

He slapped me across the cheek, jabbing an index finger into my face for emphasis. "Enemy didn't show until after the hour was up. You still owe me that case of beer."

He spun on his heels and joined the others before I could do anything beyond nod numbly. The men were now dragging the enemies' bodies into our hiding spot, pushing and kicking them into the undergrowth.

The only decision left to be made was which direction to move, and Sergio didn't bother asking for my opinion.

"Due west two hundred meters before evasive maneuvers," he whispered to Viggs.

Then we faded into the jungle.

6

We moved quickly from the enemy contact, altering our movement to discourage pursuit. First we executed a hurried foot race in one direction, leaving obvious ground sign for trackers to follow. Then we completed a new series of evasive maneuvers before switching course and stealthily creeping away along a different route.

When we'd created enough distance from the enemy bodies and felt sure we weren't being tracked, we stopped for a rest break.

The interlocking tree canopies completely blocked out the sky and were penetrated by only the finest drizzle of sparkling sunlight that lit them just enough for me to make out their features before we turned to pull 360 security, standing nearly back-to-back. Birdcalls gradually resumed above us, soon eclipsing the sound of our panting breaths until the jungle's noise felt like a protective cocoon assuring our safety from pursuit.

Reilly was the first to whisper, "We couldn't have been that unlucky twice in forty-eight hours."

"We weren't." Sergio's voice was measured, though I could sense a tinge of disbelief as he continued, "David relayed false coordinates over the radio. The enemy confirmed the same grid to their own headquarters."

"You sure?" Viggs asked.

"I'm sure. The exact ten-digit grid, not a number off. They must have intercepted our communication."

Viggs was holding a GPS he'd taken off a body, thumbing the buttons as he shook his head. "I told you, no one's cracking the Handler's radio encryption. And this GPS I took off the dead radio operator has got five grids of interest—look familiar?"

Sergio took the GPS from him, flipped through the stored checkpoints, and sighed. "All four rope points are here—primary, alternate, contingency, and emergency. As well as the grid that David reported."

"Lucky thing," I noted, "that we switched rope points at the last minute."

"Agreed. So there must be a leak somewhere in HQ. Someone providing information to the opposition."

Reilly said tentatively, "Or David's right—"

"He's not."

"—about the Handler slating us to be killed out here."

"Impossible. We've got over a decade of Outfit service between us. Multiple valor bonuses. There's another explanation. There has to be."

I shook my head. "We're all expendable to the Handler, I assure you. And mine is the only explanation for our pursuers having the same grid I transmitted, whether you want to admit it or not."

Cancer tossed a pocket-sized notebook and folded map toward Sergio and me. "I pulled these off the commander's body. Maybe they have our answer."

Sergio took the notebook and flipped the pages in quick succession. I unfolded the map. It was an outdated local version of the razor-sharp, recently mapped graphics that we used to navigate. But to our enemy's credit, the map was completely clean—not a single man-drawn marking of any kind.

"Map is sterilized," I said. "Same as ours."

Sergio lowered the notepad, shaking his head. "Notebook is pretty clean. Just notes about logistics, radio frequencies, all in Spanish. What else did we recover off the dead?"

Viggs replied, "I disabled the radio, but it was too heavy to take with us. And other than the sterilized GPS, the bodies I searched were pretty clean. No pocket litter."

"Same," Cancer agreed, "except that map and the notebook."

"I got nothing," Reilly murmured, almost to himself. I looked to him as I tucked the map away in my kit, feeling a collective frustrated silence fall over us.

Something was off with Reilly. He had pulled the fighting knife from his kit and was running his fingers down the flat side of the blade with a faraway look in his eyes. Dirt caked his hands and was embedded beneath his fingernails. Uncountable tiny thorn cuts marred his knuckles. But Reilly continued stroking the clean blade with his fingertips, his thoughts lost somewhere else. On something he wasn't saying, I thought. What could it be?

There was more to Reilly than met the eye. I remembered what he'd said to me shortly after we met in Rio: *We all go to war together before the Outfit, and now some criminals who've never gone to combat tell us not to talk to each other while we go die for their operation.*

And that was the Organization's power—the cultish codes of silence, the harsh retributions, the threats and disavowal of captured shooters. At its best, the Organization produced people like Reilly, who begrudgingly obeyed; at its worst, it created fierce loyalists like Sergio.

Then my thoughts turned to the Indian, who had advised me on infiltrating the Outfit to kill the Handler. *You are not the first I have sent. None have emerged.*

The next time I saw him, he was strapped to the electric chair with the Handler resting a hand on his shoulder, taunting him.

We had an amenable arrangement, Upraj. I pretended to believe you dead, and you funneled would-be assassins to the Outfit in the hopes that one would kill me someday.

Then Sage sprang to mind.

Think of your return from Somalia. Have you wondered why he told the Outfit he'd be arriving on the jet when it was just me? It was to draw out assassins—he is well aware there are several of them working at the Outfit. If that plane got blown up by a rocket, I'd be killed in the process. As would the assassins. Believe me when I say the Handler is not above sending me to death in the line of duty, much less you.

A final chilling thought—how easily the Handler had approved my request to lead an Outfit team in South America, overruling the adamant counsel of his daughter's bodyguard and his own Chief Vicar of Defense. There was only one reason he'd approve my demand so willingly.

I looked up and announced, "Anyone else join the Outfit to kill the Handler?"

A beat of astounded silence followed.

Sergio's head whipped toward me. "What did you say?"

"You heard me. You all did."

No one spoke.

I continued, "You've all got stage fright? Fine. I was on a paramilitary team before this. Boss's team, with Matz, Ophie, and Ian. We did some work for the Handler, and he wiped out everyone but me and Ian. Who knows the Indian?"

Silence.

"Just me? All right, the Indian set me up with an Outfit interview, said I wasn't the first he'd sent to kill the Handler. And I know for a fact there are other assassins in the Outfit—I've heard that much from the Handler himself, right before he fried the Indian in an electric chair. And if any of you *are* assassins, I assure you the Handler knows. The Indian was a legitimate resister—but the man providing his inside information was a double agent the whole time. And now I'm assigned to a team with four guys seemingly pulled at random from all over the continent. What else could we all have in common?"

Viggs shifted uncomfortably.

Sergio finally spoke again. "Enough of this treasonous drivel."

"Enough of your brainwashed hero-worship of a sociopath."

"How dare you question the Handler? You're a *kid* nominated here against the advice of everyone who could fight it, starting with me."

"Be that as it may, as long as I'm here you're going to obey my orders."

"Your orders do not supersede the sanctity of the Organization. One more word and I will forcibly take command."

"You mutiny against me, Sergio, and you better kill me outright."

He halted at my words, his eyes dropping to my rifle angled toward his head.

"You wouldn't dare—"

"Kill you out here? No, I wouldn't *prefer* to." I shrugged. "But I'll *dare* plenty."

Presently he began maneuvering his barrel slowly, subtly in my direction. I flicked my safety lever to fire, the mechanical *click* exploding in the space between my eyes and his. He froze.

I said, "End of the line, Sergio. Choose now whether you're alive or dead."

I heard the others move around me, though whether in support of Sergio or me I couldn't tell, and I couldn't break my focus to find out—if I removed my eyes from Sergio, I was dead.

"The choice is not yours," Sergio hissed. "There are four of us who aren't *traitors* to this Organization."

"My finger is on the trigger. If one of them touches me right now, they kill us both. Think hard about what you want to do here, Sergio."

His arms tensed around his weapon, and I started to take the slack out of my trigger.

"Fuck it," Reilly announced. "I'm here to kill the Handler."

Sergio swung his head toward Reilly, his eyes ablaze with disbelief.

Reilly shrugged apathetically. "Don't look at me like that. David's the sanest person I've talked to since joining the Outfit. And we both ended up there for the same reason." His eyes ticked toward me. "Sorry about your team. I met Boss once. He was tight with my team leader, Jimmy."

My mind flashed back to the first time I met Ian during the hotel room mission brief, when he'd warned us about the Handler: *Jimmy's team dropped off the map last week.*

"Your team went missing last summer, right?" I asked. "Ian was our intel guy. He warned Boss about it."

"Yeah," Reilly agreed. "A little different with us,

though. We finished our last job. Jimmy had set up a safe house in Belize, didn't tell anyone outside our team. Every man had his own route there. I was the only one who made it. Couple guys rolled me up and delivered me to the Indian."

"And the Indian made you the same deal as me."

Reilly nodded slowly.

Cancer sighed. "All right, assholes. We met the Indian too."

"Your team?"

"Naw." He shook his head with a half-smile. "Me and Viggs here."

I looked to Viggs to see if this was a joke, and instead saw the embarrassment on his face.

"You've got to be shitting me. Same team?"

"Yeah," Viggs admitted.

"So...what? The rest of your guys get wiped out or what?"

Cancer corrected me. "No, we all made it to the Dominican Republic. But we heard about Jimmy's and Boss's teams. Me and Viggs decided to do something 'bout it, started asking around and met the Indian."

"What about the rest of your team?"

"They're still safe. Relocated after me and Viggs left, but they're alive somewhere."

"Why didn't you stay with them?"

Viggs turned toward me with a half shrug. "Retirement got boring."

I nodded. This was a masterstroke by the Handler: he'd honored his terms to me by granting my assignment request, and had done so in front of his daughter. Then he'd consolidated all his would-be assassins and sent us off to certain death, disposing of his trash in one fell swoop. This entire operation was a suicide mission in its purest form.

My entire team had intended to kill the Handler —except one.

I swung my head to Sergio. "So what's your excuse? If you're not an assassin, how did you end up here?"

Sergio didn't answer.

I hadn't seen him lose focus or waver in the slightest since we launched on this mission—hell, since he'd supervised my admission into the Outfit—and now he appeared to be lost in troubled thought, practically in shock.

I persisted, "Spit it out, old man. I remember Sage saying you'd blown one chance to meet the Handler, and you wouldn't get another. What did that mean?"

He didn't look at me. He didn't look at anyone. His eyes were directed at the ground between us, unfocused.

"I earned an assignment to the Mist Palace," he said quietly. "Two years ago. But the night before my promotion, one of my recruits was found to be an assassin. He was reported when he tried to make contact with others in the Outfit...but not by me. The investigation found me innocent of involvement in the assassination plot but negligent in failing to detect it. I lost the promotion."

He blinked his vision clear, looking to me. "And now, I'm here."

And that explained it all, I thought. Sergio's overdeveloped sense of loyalty to the Organization, his adamant denial that the Handler had sent us here to die. His every effort since I'd met him had been an attempt at redemption...and now, the testimony of every teammate was forcing him to accept that the Handler wanted him dead regardless.

Before I could respond, Reilly's hand clamped onto my arm. "Listen."

I fell silent, hearing birdcalls quieting to our north. In the distance, someone was approaching.

Sergio's posture stiffened abruptly. "Let's move," he whispered. "Viggs, take point."

FREEDOM

Nulla tenaci invia est via

For the tenacious, no road is impassable

7

We successfully outpaced whichever element had been approaching our position, the usual jungle sounds continuing unabated until thunder rumbled to our east. Shortly before sunset, we took a ninety-degree dogleg off our route and selected a thicket to use as our bed-down site. A cloud of mosquitos descended upon us as we set up our perimeter, once again placing a Claymore mine to cover our back trail.

We could hear the chatter of insects fall silent as a distant wave of rainfall washed over them. By the time we settled in to rest in shifts as we had the previous night, the snarl of thunder was rolling overhead. Pattering raindrops began to fall angrily through the treetops, audibly rattling in the leaves above us for a few minutes before we felt the first water on our skin. The mosquitos vanished—a welcome reprieve for which we'd pay instead with water-logged hands and feet. The jungle would take its pound of flesh either way.

Little was said as we arranged ponchos over ourselves and our rucks. The now steady rainfall made it too difficult to hear each other whisper. Despite the physical strain of our second day on patrol, the revelation that we were nearly all would-be assassins of the Handler made sleep near impossible.

Instead I sat, feeling the beads of rain ticking against my poncho hood as my mind raced. I'd known there were others like me in the Outfit's ranks...now we were together, and I was in charge. We were a literal and metaphorical representation of those who stood against the Handler—well, except for Sergio—and now we'd been found out. No, that wasn't accurate. We'd been *assembled* by virtue of the threat we posed, a unity that would be empowering if it hadn't required us to be condemned in the process.

It was easy to be flippant about my own survival, a skill I'd earned if not outright forged over the past few years. But I wasn't going to lose another team, not after Boss, Matz, and Ophie. I wasn't going to let the Handler win, not after Karma.

But how could I achieve any other fate?

Eventually I lost consciousness. But it was a restless sleep soon plagued by a dream, one I'd had before, with fleeting images of a ship being tossed in a nighttime storm at sea. Flickers of intermittent lightning preceded total blackness just as they had both times the dream had come before—the night before Boss's team died, and the night before I killed Jais. This time I *knew* I was dreaming, sensed the significance and wanted to rouse myself awake, to break the curse—yet I couldn't. I was powerless to move my body or direct my mind away from the ship over-turning in a giant surging wave. And when the next flash of lightning streaked across the sky, shards of wooden planks and tattered sails floated up from the frothy, shifting ocean surface.

When the lightning flashed again, the ocean was gone.

I was on the ground in Rio, blood oozing from my gunshot wounds, looking up at the man who shot me. Only this time it was Agustin, holding a smoking gun as he watched me kindly, tilting his bearded face to observe my suffering. I searched for a gun on the ground beside me, but there was only Agustin standing over me. I tried to speak but could only utter hollow gasps.

Agustin grinned at this, pointing his gun at my face. Then his head jerked upright as if he'd heard something. But after a moment he relaxed, shrugging and aiming at me again. His features were calm, almost trancelike as he spoke the last five words I'd ever hear.

Do you see our Redeemer?

Then he shot me, the sound too loud for any gun of dreaming or even waking hours—it was the blast of a Claymore explosion.

I awoke to total darkness, the detonating mine's blast replaced by an assault rifle firing in automatic bursts and Sergio shouting.

"BREAK CONTACT!"

I heaved myself forward, pulling my body a few feet from the center of the formation as we split down the middle. Viggs was shooting—he had been closest to the Claymore. I clicked the knob on my night vision, and the jungle appeared in murky green hues. Viggs's magazine went empty, and Sergio opened fire. I saw Viggs run down the center of our two ranks, racing away from the gunfire.

Struggling to a knee, I took aim in the direction Sergio was shooting. The tension was incredible as I resisted the urge to fire; finally, Sergio's weapon went silent.

Then I blasted short automatic bursts into the night, spreading them left to right around the Claymore position. Sergio ran behind me, sprinting after Viggs.

Streaks of neon green zipped through the forest—

tracer rounds of the enemy returning fire. I directed my fire toward their origin, pumping dozens of rounds at an unsustainable rate.

When my weapon clicked empty, Reilly immediately filled the void with automatic fire as I stood and ran behind him. Cancer was the last man. I caught a glimpse of him preparing his time-delay Claymore mine—in sixty seconds our bed-down location would turn into a blast aimed at our hunters.

I plunged into the dark jungle and ran down a thin line of trampled ferns where Viggs and Reilly had broken trail. Gunfire continued behind me—had Reilly spent his magazine and been replaced by Cancer yet? I couldn't tell. Enemy gunfire was increasing in volume, swallowing the sound of the jungle rain and replacing it with chaos. Fluorescent green tracer rounds sparked around me, zinging through the trees as if trying to light my way. I reloaded my weapon on the move, hearing a machinegun open fire. Its rope of blaze orange tracers cut down the jungle to my left.

Suddenly the gunfire ended altogether.

By my estimate I was approaching a hundred meters of straight-line rush, moving as fast as the jungle would allow and praying I was on Viggs and Sergio's trail. A blinding flash of sun lit the forest and immediately went dark as an ear-shattering BOOM washed over me from behind. I tried to blink my view clear, sweeping my night vision left to right. Was this a trail broken by men—or was the correct trail to my right?

I threaded my way between vegetation, but the ground around me was becoming more open and, therefore, more difficult to discern human passage. With the poor illumination and rain, it became virtually impossible.

I stopped to listen but couldn't hear anything through the pelting raindrops.

Knowing I had at least another fifty meters until we were supposed to consolidate, I raced forward, hoping I had chosen correctly.

I was considering turning on my FM radio to contact them when I caught sight of a faint, pulsing glow through the leaves ahead. Turning my head to the side, I saw that the light vanished outside of my night vision—an infrared strobe, partially shielded so it would be undetectable unless you were extremely close.

Moving toward it, I found Viggs and Sergio back-to-back in the darkness, pulling security. The strobe was blinking softly on the ground, its flash obscured by Viggs's boonie cap over it. I knelt beside them, placing my ruck against theirs as we adjusted orientation to divide sectors of fire.

"You guys good?" I asked.

"We're fine," Sergio said. I suspended relief until the other two had linked up—if we had to transport an injured man in the present circumstances, we'd be in bad shape indeed.

Sergio continued, "When we've got everyone, we need to move due south another two hundred meters quick as we can. Then we'll start evasion. After daybreak, we'll find someplace we can hole up and find the device."

"What device?" I asked.

"Think about it," Sergio said. "They just found us at night, and practically tripped over our goddamn Claymore. Someone planted a tracking device on our kit."

Of course. We'd covered significant distance before bedding down for the night. The rain would've washed away our ground sign by now, and our enemies couldn't have followed it in the dark regardless. This time we weren't being compromised by either our radio or dogs.

I muttered, "Oh...shit."

Viggs said, "It's all right, boss. Triple canopy jungle doesn't allow constant tracking—only periodic transmissions when there's less overhead cover. We'll have time to evade."

"You sure?"

"Positive," Viggs said in a cheery voice. "Otherwise, we'd be dead already." He partially uncovered his strobe before shielding it again. I heard Reilly crashing toward us.

Reilly appeared and fell into position. "Anyone injured?"

"No," Sergio replied. "We're toting a tracking device, though. We need distance and daylight before we shake our gear down to find it."

"Oh...shit," he said.

Cancer approached soon thereafter, his figure threading a path through the falling rain. He was moving quickly, no indication of injury, and Viggs killed the strobe as soon as it was apparent Cancer had seen us. We stood without speaking as Cancer rejoined our ranks with a single, harshly whispered declaration.

"We just pissed off the bear, boys."

Viggs led us due south, picking up the pace as much as the terrain allowed. We spread out in a file as we distanced ourselves from one another while keeping sight of the man to our front.

In a split second, the rain stopped. Visibility improved drastically without the streaks of rain obscuring our night vision, and for a brief time we were able to break into a shuffling jog.

* * *

The storm had wreaked havoc on the forest floor. Terrain that was easily negotiable when dry became a spongy, soggy trap of muddy earth that swallowed our soles, interspersed with rocks so slick they prevented our boots from gaining purchase.

We were truly masterless now, animals fleeing for survival. Our movement continued for one purpose only: to find someplace to hide so we could locate the tracking device. There was nothing else. No Outfit objective to reconnoiter, no headquarters to take guidance from.

And no way out.

That last prospect troubled me through hours of movement that ranged from walking to jogging as the terrain and visibility permitted. It was an endless cycle, mirroring our mission. Move stealthily, get compromised, run for our lives. Then move stealthily again. Only now the stakes were higher. Every hour that passed without us calling headquarters built suspicion that we'd gone fully rogue, which carried with it the implication that we'd figured out the Handler was trying to kill us. Difficult odds under the best of circumstances, worse yet with half the world hunting us.

What could we do from here? I tried to think how to extricate my team from this situation. This was the Triple Frontier, the eye of a chaotic hurricane of crime and terror. Given the choice of Brazil, Paraguay, and Argentina, Ribeiro's remaining staff had chosen the least developed corner—the Argentinian jungle. Why had they done so? And what could we leverage to get ourselves out?

The area was free of urban development, and with it the specter of constant surveillance. They'd chosen this wilderness for the same reason we'd ostensibly been sent as a ground reconnaissance team—because the jungle canopy prevented aerial observation. With strict discipline and the use of primitive communications methods, one could practically disappear out here.

Except for my team, despite our best efforts. Once we found and disposed of any tracking devices, we still had to figure out our next play. Overland movement was a poor exit strategy from this death sentence: it would take us weeks of patrol to cover the ground, living off the land or what we could steal before reaching civilization. But being in the jungle didn't mean being alone. Hundreds if not thousands of illicit men and women had taken to this frontier for the same reason as Ribeiro. I knew from both Ian and the mission brief that the jungle hid terrorist training camps, abandoned cocaine processing labs, and unregulated airstrips.

My mind seized on that last point: airstrips. I almost wanted to ask if anyone on the team could fly a plane, but I couldn't risk revealing the extent of my despair. If we could find an aircraft, we could find a pilot. While we lacked any fistfuls of cash to speak of, a pilot could nonetheless be properly motivated to do our bidding with the aid of a gun barrel to his temple. It didn't matter what cartel or terror network we pissed off in the process, because they were all after us anyway.

We moved through the first hues of sunrise, the vivid green night vision brightening until the naked eye could see. I stripped the device off my head and the cycle continued—murky green hues cast in natural light, brightening in color with the sun's ascent. To our right, densely clustered formations of muddy stone threaded uphill, a single stream of water penetrating the gaps to form a trickling waterfall that sprayed across the final two feet of open space into a murky pool.

"Kill one, fill one," Sergio whispered. "Make it fast."

We took turns on security, each man downing a canteen and passing it to Reilly so he could refill it from the waterfall. I glanced at the others.

Patterns of raised insect bites now covered our exposed skin. Where one bite ended, the next began; the result was the appearance of round reptilian scales across necks and wrists. By then we'd long since stopped using camouflage sticks and instead smeared the ample mud across our faces and necks, creating a caked surface of mottled brown, cream, and rust that made us look more monster than man.

We were all going hungry, having rationed our food supply following the first enemy contact. While we'd planned for a thirty-six-hour mission, we could only stuff so much food in rucks already overfull with water, ammo, explosives, and extra radio batteries. Even then our field rations would have done little more than sustain us over the course of a normal recon mission. Given the extra energy expenditure of multiple gunfights and fleeing enemy contact, we'd finish this thing on the brink of starvation under the best of circumstances.

I focused on a single dry leaf, seemingly suspended midair before my eyes. In reality it hung inverted from the delicate tendril of an invisible spider web, slowly rotating from some imperceptible disturbance in the air. My fatigued mind was entranced.

"Come on, Suicide," Reilly whispered, waving a hand for my canteen. Then he jumped slightly at the sting of some unseen insect, slapping at his exposed neck.

As I handed him my canteen, I saw an impossibly large catfish drifting beneath the surface of the pool, wriggling its way through the mild current. I had a brief memory of returning from Rio with a pistol hidden in my arm sling, walking over the bridge in the garden and glancing at a fish swimming in the water below. That fish was the Handler's pet as much as I was, as much as we all were.

I felt nauseous.

The Handler had to die. For what he did to Boss's team, for what he did to us now. Yet there was seemingly no way to stop him, no secret of which he was unaware or gap in his armor big enough to slip through like the falling stream of water passing through the rocks beside me.

We continued marching, unable to find a suitably concealed place for us to strip off our gear for a thorough search. Another hour passed before we saw it—the hiding spot to end all hiding spots. A gnarled, tangled cowlick of thorn-strewn brush on the side of a steep hill. This swath of dark jungle was far from water sources and removed from easily passable terrain. Once we clawed and fought our way into it, I thought, we'd be invisible.

Sergio said, "Before we commit to this, I want to do a quick walk-around. Find our outs."

A short patrol revealed this natural hiding spot to exist in a small bowl in the side of a hill, easily escapable down-hill. Leaving via the uphill route was more difficult but still doable over a natural crest running seventy-five meters along the high ground.

Once we had a full understanding of our escape routes, we began crawling through the tangled under-growth. Maneuvering into the thick brush like a hunted deer diving into thicket too dense for hunters to pursue, we finally settled into a tight circle and began stripping off our gear to search for tracking devices.

The act felt alien, nearly self-destructive. After days on the run, we were isolating ourselves and removing every item needed to shoot and survive—every bit of it Outfit-issued. And we were doing so with the full knowledge that one or more tracking devices had been periodically broadcasting our location to get here. But there was no other way. We needed to be stationary in dense cover just to survive long enough to search our kit.

And search we did. Each man tore his gear apart, meticulously probing every pocket and seam.

I poured the contents of my rucksack and began rifling through them, whispering to the others, "We all agree those guys who hit our patrol base were a new enemy force?"

Sergio was patting down the back of his chest rig now lying on the ground before him. "Without a doubt. We haven't encountered much more than a dozen guys before, but that machinegun means it was a platoon-sized element at least."

"And they were good," Viggs added. "Used the rain to cover the sound of their patrol. Moving at night in this weather means they were well-trained and had the night vision to back them up."

Cancer was reaching into the now-empty pockets of his rucksack, feeling for anything out of place. "The dog team hit us dead-on because they had our actual grid—we'd just sent that radio transmission from the open." He flipped his ruck over and began probing the back padding for anything that had been sewn in. "But the second team came across us where there was thick overhead cover, remember? You barely made radio contact through the trees, and the only thing the enemy knew was the location that you reported. They didn't have tracker confirmation. Guys last night *only* had tracker confirmation, because we didn't report shit else. Whoever they were, I think the Handler's holding their strings."

I followed Cancer's lead, pressing against my ruck's back pads.

Feeling a dense mass beneath one pad, I whipped out my knife and sliced it open at the seam, then withdrew the object hidden within.

"I got one," I said, holding it aloft for all to see. It was about the size of a cigarette pack, though only a fraction of the thickness. A tiny red light blinked beside a kill switch.

I clicked the kill switch, and the red light died at once.

Sergio grunted in disapproval. "Everyone, hurry up and finish checking your kit."

The team continued searching, each man putting his gear back together once he was satisfied.

I asked, "Think we should turn the tracker on and leave it in the open as a diversion? Could give us some lead time."

"Bad idea," Viggs replied, throwing his chest rig back over his shoulders.

"Why?"

"The Organization has been tracking periodic beacon transmissions. If it starts beaming continuously from one spot all of a sudden, they'll know it's a decoy."

Reilly stuffed the contents of his ruck back inside. "Then we put it in a waterproof bag and send it down the river."

"If we put it in the river," Viggs warned, "it'll be moving too fast to be convincing. Besides, right now we haven't reported—could mean we haven't been able to establish comms. But if they know we've found the tracker, they'll know we've gone rogue. And once we're off the reservation, there's no way back on it. Just keep that thing turned off for now."

We continued putting our kit on as Reilly spoke, sounding frustrated. "They're going to find out we're rogue eventually. What's the point to any of this? Even if we beat every force they throw at us, the Handler will kill us anyway. We can't make it back from South America no matter what we do."

My thoughts drifted back to Ian's words. The most important part, he'd said.

If you could blow off a mission abort and still come out of Saamir's building alive, then you can make it back from South America.

Ian wasn't one to give false hope. There was a way back; he'd found it and passed it to me. Somehow.

"There's got to be a way," I declared.

"Sure," Cancer said, "if we win the war."

My mind jarred back to Ian being hoisted up from his chair by the guards. *You've got a war to win.*

"Cancer," I asked, "what's that supposed to mean?"

He shrugged. "I mean, we kill Ribeiro, war's over, right? All we gotta do is make it to North Africa and find him."

Cancer's words gave me pause. He was right, of course. What he said about winning the war by finding Ribeiro was obvious, at least in theory.

If so, Ian would have known that—and planned for it. Was that the meaning of his message?

I pulled out my map and scanned it. I tried to think, but it was hard—hunger and exhaustion were overwhelming me. My body felt like it was consuming itself. But I could only make one leap of logic based off the facts, and it didn't make sense to me.

Was Ribeiro *here*?

Everyone speculated that Ribeiro fled the continent, most likely to North Africa. What if he didn't flee at all—what if he went to ground in the jungle, and let the war rage around him?

If that was true, what would Ian do? Certainly not volunteer that information to help the Handler, whom Ian hated as much as any man alive. And he would have feared becoming expendable once he'd achieved the crowning task in his assignment of targeting Ribeiro's executive network.

Ian would have known what Cancer had just figured out—the impossible solution of killing Ribeiro, winning the war, and leaving the Handler no choice but to publicly acknowledge my team's accomplishment.

Which wouldn't be so impossible *if* Ribeiro was in the area to which Ian knew I'd be deployed. And in that event, Ian would code a message for me, would have constructed it so carefully that it risked being incomprehensible even to me. That was the meaning of Ian's dream—the one where Saamir was still in his office, alive.

"Ribeiro is here," I announced.

The team looked beyond skeptical. Sergio asked, "What do you mean, 'here?'"

"I mean right here. Within striking distance. All we have to do is find him."

Then I explained the events as I understood them—how Ian had been enslaved in the Handler's Intelligence Directorate, how he'd been promoted to targeting Ribeiro's executive network. I concluded with the mention that Ian and I were granted a five-minute meeting under surveillance that had ended with Ian assuring me I could make it back from South America.

Viggs watched me intently. "What did Ian say to you, exactly?"

I closed my eyes, visualizing the interrogation room, the guards standing over us, Ian across the table from me.

"He talked about the threats in the area—cartels, Hezbollah. The only thing I didn't need to worry about was cocaine labs, since they'd all been decommissioned when production moved out of the area. Then he talked about the paramilitary teams that worked for the Handler, how all of them had been lost after our last mission, when we killed the Handler's domestic opposition. All except one: Boss's team, because he and I were still alive."

Reilly nodded. "So one of the cocaine labs is still active."

"How do you figure that?"

Reilly gave me and then the others an incredulous look, like we all should have arrived at the same conclusion already.

Upon seeing no recognition, Reilly shook his head. "Come on, am I the only guy who majored in literature before dropping out? It's metaphor, man."

"Start talking," Cancer ordered.

Reilly shrugged. "Lots of threats in the area like Hezbollah and the cartels, but the one thing we didn't need to worry about was cocaine labs. So, one exception to the many. Lots of paramilitary teams that used to work for the Handler, but only Boss's team remains active. Again, one exception to the many, meaning there's one 'active' cocaine lab out of the many that used to be operational."

"Maybe," I mused.

Sergio nodded to me. "David, what else?"

"Then Ian talked about the first mission I did for Boss's team. The target's name was Saamir, and Ian had been having dreams that Saamir was still alive, hiding in the office where I killed him. Which I take to mean Ribeiro is still in this area, hiding."

"Maybe," Sergio conceded. "What else? The rest of the message had to be code for a specific location."

"He talked about the mission to kill Saamir. An assassination in a high-rise. Security was alerted, and Boss gave the mission abort. I disobeyed and killed the target anyway, then shot my way to the roof so I could parachute off the building and escape."

"And?"

"And Ian said that the time between those two events was the most scared he'd ever been for an operative. In hindsight, the most memorable event of his career."

"The time between those two events..."

"And he said no matter how bad things get down here, to keep hope. That if I could blow off a mission abort and still come out of Saamir's building alive, then I could make it back from South America."

Sergio held up two fingers. "The events are disobeying the abort and parachuting off the roof. Saamir was alive in the space between them. So Ribeiro is too."

"Meaning?"

Cancer interjected, "You said it was a high-rise, dumbass. What floor did you abort on?"

"The abort came when I was closing on the target's office." I thought back. "Thirty-second floor."

Viggs asked, "And what floor did you jump from?"

I thought back to my initial brief, the planning considerations I'd made for that BASE jump. "Building was thirty-eight stories."

"You sure?"

"I'm positive. I planned for a 380-foot jump, and the rule of thumb is ten feet for every story—"

"Whatever," Reilly cut me off. "So, thirty-two and

thirty-eight. The space between thirty-two and thirty-eight —a grid?"

"No," Sergio said, unfolding his map in its waterproof case and spreading it between us. "Not in our area of operations."

"Check everything with a number—anything Ian could have known."

We pored over every laminated scrap of paper and mission reference we had. But modern numbering systems had precious little use for two-digit identifiers. Most of our sequences were instead three to ten digits: numbered areas of interest, radio frequencies, latitude and longitude.

Suddenly Viggs announced, "Hilltops!"

He jabbed a finger at Sergio's map. "This map uses two-digit hilltop designations. And look here—Hill 32, and Hill 38."

Sergio grimaced. "That's got to be five klicks of rainforest, mostly swamp. It'd take us a week to cover that. And some of those coke labs in the jungle are small enough that unless you walk into them, you can walk right by without noticing."

"Well," I offered, "what choice do we have?"

Cancer snatched the map. "Christ, you guys are dumb. Look right here—Hill 32 and Hill 39 are less than a klick and a half apart. Forget the case of beer. I got a *paycheck* that says our lab is in the low ground between them. Who wants to take that bet?"

"I do," I said. "That's Hill 39. Not 38."

"Don't you welch on me, Suicide. Your buddy said the time between your mission abort and your *jump*, you dick idiot. You didn't jump from the thirty-eighth floor, you jumped from the roof. Thirty-nine."

A wave of euphoria washed over me. "Jesus," I whispered, "that's brilliant. There it is."

Reilly shook his head. "We might be missing the point. Even if Ribeiro is here, why kill him? We could switch sides. Join Ribeiro and kill the Handler."

"Ribeiro's organization," Viggs dismissed, "is too degraded from the war."

"Well what about disappearing down here? Abandon the Outfit and find a place to live."

Sergio replied this time. "If Ribeiro isn't where we think he is, we'll have to do just that. Consider it a solid Plan B."

"Enough," I said. "Ian knew more about our situation than we do now. He didn't send a code to escape or switch sides." I decided not to mention my ties to Parvaneh, which rendered both options unfavorable to me personally. "Instead, Ian sent a code to find Ribeiro and kill him against all odds, just like I did with Saamir."

Sergio nodded. "Then that's our best course of action." He pointed to the map. "We still need to cross the river. Closest bridge is here. If we get moving now, we might be able to make it across by nightfall."

Viggs was visibly cringing now. "That would take us back the way we've come."

"Who cares?" Reilly said. "They'll never expect it."

"It's not about whether they'll expect it; it's about the larger enemy elements that are following on the heels of the scout teams we've encountered. Someone mustered up an enemy platoon last night to try and bang us while we slept. If three dozen men with night vision were the closest force available with a few hours' notice, what do you think is coming a day or two behind them?"

Cancer was smiling. "We're popular right now, boys. Plenty of killing left to do."

"Well," I said to no one in particular, "when you're facing certain death, the prospect of extremely likely death becomes somewhat more appetizing, no?"

A high-pitched *thump* rang out below us, and in one terrifying second my eyes met Sergio's. We both knew what the sound was; hell, we all did. But there was nonetheless a pause of disbelief as we simultaneously hoped our ears had deceived us, which was shattered almost immediately when a half-dozen identical chirping noises followed the first sound.

We hit the deck as one, dropping as flat as we could with the recognition that 40mm grenade rounds were seconds from impacting.

They exploded in the thick overhead cover, pelting us with a shower of tiny branches. By the second volley of grenade rounds it became apparent that the enemy couldn't kill us this way—our natural cover was simply too dense, causing the rounds to detonate high above us.

"All right," I said, "here's the play: we make it to the crossing point, and go hit Ribeiro. Then report to HQ."

Reilly asked, "How we supposed to get out of this?"

I shrugged. "No idea. That's Sergio's job."

Sergio rolled his eyes. "One of us will offset from the others, remove his suppressor, and make some noise. Rest of us climb the hill, shoot a gap as silently as we can. Then we run."

"Good," I agreed.

"Noise diversion is the most dangerous part," he continued. "One man will have to work his way to us, alone."

"I'll do it."

"We need experience, not enthusiasm. Viggs."

Viggs was already releasing the latch on his rifle

suppressor, forcing the locking mechanism counterclockwise on its threads before yanking it off. "I'm on it."

"Turn your radio on. I'll key the mic twice for you to initiate. If we can do this thing silently, I'll make comms and guide you through." Viggs nodded, and Sergio directed his gaze to the rest of us. "Reilly on point. We're going to punch a hole in the line, drop every shithead in our path simultaneously. And for the love of Christ, keep it quiet. Any noise endangers Viggs. Questions?"

After a beat, Sergio looked to Viggs. "You're still here?"

Viggs moved out to the western edge of the brush. The rest of us pushed uphill toward the enemy perimeter we knew awaited us on the ridge. The men beside me were resolute, moving confidently with newfound purpose; we simply felt this would work.

We tried to get the jump on the enemy at once, just as Sergio had said. In a vacuum it would have been possible to surprise and kill them with well-timed suppressed fire. Out here in the bush, we should have known better—the same abundance of tangled branches and trees that made our hiding spot a recon man's dream likewise made it a nightmare to fight through. The jungle was agnostic; it would absorb and deflect bullets fired from either side, though in the current context it played out to our enemies' advantage rather than ours.

The end result was chaos.

* * *

We crept forward as stealthily as we could, which, given the tangled undergrowth all around us, meant agonizingly slow progress.

It wasn't just the foliage slowing us, though. Knowing that

contact was imminent, we moved through the undergrowth like jungle cats, swiveling our heads and directing our sight and hearing to the slightest indication of an enemy presence. Each step was a slow, methodical foot placement lest we snap a twig. When Reilly paused for the slightest moment, all of us froze. Our M4s were probing extensions of our razor-sharp awareness, following the movement of our eyes as we scanned for any indication of men we had to kill silently.

By that point in the mission we were hardwired to one another's body language and facial expressions; either spoke as loud as a verbal report. Reilly, on point, tensed with his first enemy sighting. His hand signal told the rest: *three fighters*. We relayed the message and, seeing that Reilly remained in place, pushed forward through the brush alongside him. Sergio noiselessly keyed his radio twice, transmitting twin bursts of static that triggered Viggs's unsuppressed automatic fire to our left.

The barking rounds incited a rustle of movement to our front as fighters repositioned themselves toward the noise. By now Sergio, Cancer, and I were spaced out along Reilly's flank, and we moved forward as a single line, providing each man with clear fields of fire.

Our four suppressed rifles were probing through the brush, and I caught sight of two enemy fighters wearing tiger-stripe jungle fatigues, their faces turned to the sound of Viggs's fire to reveal profiles of matching ethnic features. These men were Arab and armed with rifles that I couldn't make out through the leaves—where was the third enemy?

One of their faces flicked toward us, and Reilly fired a subsonic round that caught the man's nose with a dull *thwack*.

Sergio and I ripped near-simultaneous shots at the second man. His face crumpled as the bullets split exit wounds through the back of his skull. Both men vanished in the brush and Reilly was now racing forward, trying to get a bead on the third.

The rest of us fought through the brush alongside him, following his lead. Cancer opened fire at someone I couldn't see, then fell backwards as a burst of automatic rifle fire exploded to our front—whether he'd fallen to dodge a rifle or been cut down, I couldn't tell.

Everything else was a blur. Reilly, Sergio, and I thrashed forward to slay the offending shooter. I cleared a tree to find two men just meters beyond, sweeping the bushes with bayonet-pointed assault rifles. Sergio shot one in the shoulder as Reilly and I engaged the other. By the time Sergio emptied his magazine into his wounded enemy, the man was lunging directly toward me in the throes of death.

I sidestepped, but the bayonet sliced across my right forearm, splitting my sleeve as his weight bowled me over. My hand dropped my rifle in a spasmodic jerk, and I crashed to the ground beside the dead man as more fighters spilled into the killing ground.

Scrambling for my weapon, I saw Sergio fire the last round in his magazine before tackling an enemy fighter. I snatched my rifle, rolled back against my ruck, and blasted a man trading shots with Reilly. Swinging my aim toward a flash of movement, I saw Cancer firing his SR-25 sniper rifle off the shoulder, looking over the sights toward an enemy entrenched somewhere in the bushes.

I dropped my barrel to Sergio. The fighter he'd tackled was now atop him, trying to crush his face by driving a rifle downward. I tried for a single headshot, but my bullet ripped through the enemy's throat instead. Blood spewed across Sergio's face as he rolled the enemy over and drew his knife for the kill.

Bullets were everywhere, zinging and hissing through the brush. Debris from bark and branches tumbled around us. By now I was on a knee, looking for targets, when a man crashed out of the brush beside me—he didn't see me until he'd knocked me down, falling atop me in the process. His weight descended on my chest as I pushed him off with my rifle. The man rolled away on his side, his bayonet tipped toward my chest as he took aim quicker than I could.

Viggs burst out of the brush at that moment, almost running over top of us. He drove an instinctive kick into the enemy's rifle, deflecting the bayonet away from me. But as Viggs regained his footing, the man pirouetted his rifle and speared it upward at him.

I didn't have time to see if the bayonet connected or not—I scrambled atop the man, knocking his rifle aside before he could fire. Clawing the sides of his head with both hands, I drove my thumbs into his eyes.

The action incited a horrible shrieking cry that turned my blood to ice. His body rocked in spasms so violent that I struggled to stay atop him. He wasn't going to die this way, and the screaming was unbearable.

Powerful hands ripped me off the man, tossing me to the side. Viggs stood over the enemy, who was now clutching his face in horror. In a swift motion, Viggs drove an M4 barrel into the screaming mouth and blasted a short automatic burst. The shots canoed the man's head completely apart, and his shrieking stopped at last.

Viggs helped me up with one hand, and I took in the sight before us.

Bodies were everywhere, mounds of tiger-stripe fatigues soaked in blood. Cancer was moving among them, methodically dispatching survivors with his knife. Reilly was already emplacing a time-delay Claymore mine. Sergio's face was a slick of black arterial blood from the man I'd shot off him, his eyes white and wild.

"Viggs," he said, pointing beyond the fighting perimeter. Then he lowered his eyes and corrected himself. "Reilly, take point."

"One minute to detonation," Reilly replied, leaving his Claymore in place. He stood and charged off in the direction that Sergio pointed, and Cancer followed behind him. It was my turn next. I reloaded on the move, seeing a look of consternation on Sergio's face that seemed unrelated to the massacre.

Taking a final look back at the carnage, I felt all the elation drain out of me in one devastating second.

Viggs was following me, one hand gripping his rifle, the other pressed to his abdomen, where blood oozed between his fingers. He looked at me with a strained expression, face pale but voice unwavering.

"Don't sweat this, boss. Just get us to Ribeiro."

I turned and pushed my way forward. As we moved away from the devastation on the ridge, I cast periodic rearward glances to find that somehow, against all possible odds, Viggs was keeping pace.

ENDGAME

Mortui vivos docent

The dead teach the living

8

The cycle was repeating itself. Compromise by enemy forces, break contact with extreme violence, and then evade—only this time, we no longer had a tracking device periodically broadcasting our location. That was of little consolation given that Viggs had been wounded to get us this far.

After we'd created some distance in a straight-line movement as fast as we could manage, Sergio directed us through evasive maneuvers and a change of direction. Tilting my right forearm, I examined the cut where the bayonet had sliced my sleeve apart. The skin beneath was unbroken. How was that even possible?

Adrenaline faded from my system, and with it any physical reprieve of two days' worth of jungle movement. Now I felt once again beleaguered by the constant itching of countless bug bites, the abrasion of cuts and scrapes against dirty fatigues, the endless strain of my rucksack dragging me down. But if Viggs could keep pace while wounded, I thought, then I had no cause for complaint.

We finally stopped for Reilly to treat Viggs.

I knelt beside them, astonished that Viggs wasn't

screaming in pain or passed out from shock. Nonetheless, his huge form looked strangely boyish and vulnerable as he lay flat on the ground, holding the fabric of his blood-soaked shirt to expose the injury for Reilly.

The wound was narrow—only an inch-long gaping slit in his abdomen. But the sheer volume of blood that poured down his side indicated that the bayonet had plunged deep enough to cause damage, though how severe, only Reilly could say for sure.

Reilly used a small handheld surgical stapler to close the wound. Each click-clack of the device lanced a staple through Viggs's flesh, sealing his broken skin together until a parallel row of staples closed the gash completely. Viggs was stoic throughout this process, gritting his teeth in silence until Reilly had finished. After wiping the excess blood, Reilly placed gauze atop the wound and fixed it in place with a plate-sized adhesive chest seal.

Cancer approached my side and whispered, "Didn't have much time to search bodies back there. But I found this."

He handed me a crumpled piece of notepaper, then stepped away to pull security before I could read it.

I flattened the notepaper open, seeing only a brief, crudely scrawled message. It was the kind of field note written in duplicate and given to various leaders in a patrol while they were on the move, when updates to the mission-in-progress couldn't be disseminated via a verbal brief.

The message was clear enough.

5 HOMBRES. COMANDANTE: RIVERS.

Lowering the paper in disgust, I directed my attention back to Viggs.

Reilly had inserted a saline lock into the crook of Viggs's elbow, though instead of starting an IV drip he procured a needle and drew a clear fluid into it from a small bottle.

Viggs muttered, "That for infection?"

"Nope. It's tranexamic acid," Reilly replied, injecting the needle into the saline port and depressing the plunger to launch the fluid into Viggs's bloodstream. "That'll help with blood clotting. *Now* we can deal with infection."

He filled a syringe with lidocaine, then injected it into a vial of Invanz powder. Shaking the contents until the powder had dissolved, he drew the solution into his syringe and whispered, "This one goes into your ass."

Viggs squinted at him. "You serious?"

Reilly shrugged. "Unless you want to sit here so I can run out an IV drip. You that anxious to see how quick those Hezbollah fuckers can find us again?"

Grunting, Viggs rolled onto his side and yanked one side of his pants down, exposing his buttock.

"Attaboy," Reilly said, wiping a circular area of Viggs's ass with an alcohol wipe. Then he stuck the needle into the spot, injecting the solution intramuscularly.

Viggs pulled his pants back up as Reilly sat back on his heels, satisfied.

"The good news," Reilly said with a sigh, wiping the sweat from his face with his forearm, "is that there's no damage to your liver or spleen. Bad news: your walking hours are numbered."

Viggs was struggling to his feet. I cringed with the thought of the pain he must have been fighting through at that moment, but he insisted, "I'm fine to move on my own."

"For now," Reilly agreed, packing up his medical supplies. "But you've lost a lot of blood. When it gets too painful to walk, I'm breaking out the poleless litter and we'll carry you the rest of the way."

Sergio and I briefly conferred with one another.

"One wound," Sergio whispered, "and no major organ involvement. We got off easy."

I couldn't believe how relaxed he was about the whole affair. "Yeah, but I'm worried about his mobility."

"Don't be. He's fine to make it to the crossing point. After that we're home free."

"What about when we make it to Ribeiro?"

Sergio gave a nonchalant shrug. "We change the firing line, put Viggs on the sniper rifle. Cancer maneuvers with us instead."

I nodded. Sergio was totally composed, and I decided that Viggs wasn't the first casualty he'd sustained on mission. Judging by Sergio's response, he'd pulled more than a few wounded out of life-or-death scenarios.

"One more thing," I said, handing him the notepaper. "Cancer recovered this off a body back there."

Sergio glanced at the text. *5 HOMBRES. COMAN-DANTE: RIVERS.*

"I'm a little jealous, David." Shaking his head, he crumpled the paper and shoved it in his pocket. Then he smiled at me and whispered, "We've all got a price on our heads. But you're the belle of the ball."

* * *

We headed on course another ten meters past the treatment site, then doglegged ninety degrees and began evasive maneuvers toward the river crossing point.

Viggs made it nearly an hour through the jungle before he began visibly staggering. Finally he fell, waving off assistance from Reilly. He tried to rise on his own but collapsed again.

"Reilly," I hissed, "put him on the fucking poleless."

Viggs protested, "I just need a sec."

"Get on the litter, Viggs. That's not an option."

Viggs yielded. He knew I was right; he was just too proud to accept assistance without a direct order. Looking over the others, I realized that all of them would have done the same thing in Viggs's position. They'd bear any pain for their teammates, right up until they couldn't.

Reilly unrolled the poleless litter, a stretcher-length sheet of canvas with carrying handles. We situated Viggs atop it, securing him with straps across his shins and thighs, then draped a V-shaped harness from shoulders to groin.

We had to change our movement technique—Viggs was simply too heavy for two men to carry unless they let his feet drag, creating an even more discernable back trail than we already were.

I wasn't sure our solution was much better. We settled for placing Sergio on point, his freedom from the litter mitigated by carrying Viggs's ruck over his own. The rest of us carried Viggs at the shoulders and feet, rotating clockwise at periodic intervals to shift the weight between arms.

Viggs's incapacitation dealt us a crushing blow in more ways than one. We'd essentially lost our point man and, in some regards, the very center of gravity for our team. Tactically, our movement slowed to the extent that I knew we could no longer make our crossing point by nightfall. Whereas we'd previously slipped through the jungle in a spaced-out file, his litter transport required a man on either side of him, limiting our route options and increasing our ground sign.

Yet I seemed to be the only one troubled by any of this. Sergio continued to brush off my concerns. Cancer barely acknowledged that Viggs was injured at all, outside of calling him a "fat fuck" or some equally colorful variation thereof whenever we rotated positions and hoisted the stretcher back up. Reilly's only concern was in periodically checking Viggs's wound and vital signs. Each time, Reilly seemed quite pleased that the bleeding had been stemmed, as if he were any other craftsman proud of his work.

Even Viggs himself seemed okay. His face had paled between the streaks of mud camouflage and he couldn't walk, sure. He'd just taken a bayonet through the stomach, yeah. But after Sergio told him he'd still be on the Ribeiro hit, albeit as a sniper rather than a door-kicker, Viggs seemed to largely relax. Since then he'd acted like the minor detail of having been stabbed and nearly killed to save my life was little more than an inconvenience.

It occurred to me then that nothing could break these men. Two days earlier, I'd been ready to fistfight Cancer on sight. Hell, Sergio and I were one day removed from pointing guns at one another. And yet now the cruel circumstances in which we'd found ourselves seemed to tie our team together. The Handler had thrown us into a fire, but rather than destroy us, the flames had forged a bond. Our team remained unbroken.

All it took was the hope of repatriation—as soon as we'd agreed that Ribeiro was within reach, grenade rounds had literally rained down on us without inciting panic. And now, even as my worries about the mission ahead grew with each passing step, I sensed a preternatural feeling of confidence in the others.

When it became apparent that night was closing in too fast for us to reach our crossing point, we located an area of thick brush to bed down for the night. Since we wouldn't be able to perform our usual break contact drill with Viggs incapacitated, Sergio directed the emplacement of a swath of Claymores around us. In the event we got hit, he would defend in place while Reilly, Cancer, and I got a head start hauling Viggs out.

Cancer divided the contents of Viggs's ruck, and we cross-loaded it between our own so Sergio would no longer carry two packs. We adjusted ourselves around Viggs's litter at last light, just as the familiar angry armies of mosquitos charged in to assault us with bites and the incessant whirring cry of their wings.

By then, we barely cared about the bugs. Our skin was already covered in bites, and everyone was too fatigued to get worked up. The air turned bone-chillingly cold—probably in the sixties, but we were soaked and now stationary in one hundred percent humidity. The men began to shiver in sequence, but no one seemed to care about that either.

Instead, the guys were inexplicably joking back and forth, probably in their highest spirits of the entire mission.

I vaguely listened to their whispered banter, but my thoughts kept shifting to our previous nighttime compromise—when it occurred, I'd been woken up from a dream that I'd had twice before; only now, none of us died the next day. For the first time, we'd all outlived the premonition. Did that mean we were going to get hit tonight? Or had something changed—after all, this time the dream had ended with Agustin taunting me, *Do you see our Redeemer?*

"Suicide," Reilly whispered, sounding as if he'd been trying to get my attention for a while.

"What?"

"Are you deaf, or just being your usual paranoid self and overthinking the mission?"

I considered that for a moment. "Probably a little of both."

"Pull yourself together, boss. If this team were a family, then you're the mom on anxiety meds who's afraid we're falling apart."

Sergio asked, "Then who am I?"

"Obviously, you're the abusive stepdad."

"Then you," Sergio shot back, "are the family fuck-up kid who never makes anything of himself. And Cancer—"

Reilly cut him off. "Cancer's the creepy uncle touching kids in the basement."

"Good one," I noted. "What about Viggs?"

Cancer replied, "Viggs is the kid whose only hope in life is a football scholarship. Big, strong, and stupid. Loveable, but dumber than a box of shit."

Viggs objected, "I played lacrosse."

"It's a metaphor, you moron."

* * *

I slept fitfully that night, my nerves in tatters with the anticipation of the enemy finding us.

But when Sergio awoke me, the faintest hint of morning light was beginning to permeate the trees. We recovered the Claymore mines, then resumed our patrol toward the crossing point, requiring our night vision for the first half hour to effectively carry Viggs around myriad obstacles. By the time we could see under natural light, we picked up the pace, eager to reach the crossing point. Viggs wasn't getting any lighter, and temperatures wouldn't be this comfortable until nightfall.

By some miracle, we closed in on the crossing point sooner than I thought—unopposed by enemies, behind schedule, but still quicker than we should have been capable of while moving with a casualty.

Setting Viggs down with Reilly and Cancer on security, I crouched low and followed Sergio through the brush to reconnoiter the crossing point.

Sergio stopped moving suddenly, holding up a fist. I froze as he scanned the crossing point for enemy presence. When he made eye contact with me once more, it wasn't to report a count of enemy fighters.

Instead, he gave a slight shake of his head, wincing to tell me we were safe but the outcome wasn't a positive one.

"Passable?" I whispered.

He gave another shake of his head, then stepped aside so I could assume his vantage point. I moved forward, pushing the stalks of a tall fern aside so I could see.

Sergio was right. The river was dead ahead, but we sure as shit weren't going to be able to cross it here.

The bridge was in ruins, its center now a bombed-out series of wooden shards emerging from the water. We'd hoped to pull ourselves along the wooden girders beneath the bridge's surface, but they were so demolished our only recourse would have been to swim.

My eyes darted left and right, searching for some loophole, some contradiction in his logic, desperately trying to expose some flaw in nature's iron fist that had somehow escaped Sergio's seasoned perspective.

Finally I gave up, staring across the open expanse of water with a keen sense of foreboding, of the walls closing in around us.

The river was a muted gray reflecting the low, billowing mist that churned above it. It would have been easily fordable by canoe, yet by virtue of the distance between shores I knew we'd be sliced to ribbons by automatic gunfire before making it halfway across. If that didn't happen, some spotter team would report us and we'd find a ground element waiting at the other side, killing anyone who objected and hoisting the waterlogged survivors up the muddy bank for a forced march to some jungle prison camp.

The mist underscored the hopelessness of our situation, the goddamn fog another reminder of the Handler, the Mist Palace, and the entire treacherous mix of people and egos and conspiracy that had dropped us off here to die. Like the Handler, the fog couldn't penetrate the dense rainforest.

But beyond the trees, the fog roamed free. It swirled across the sky and landscape, remaining just above the treetops so that it could expose rather than conceal us.

Sergio whispered, "What's the matter with you?" I glanced back to see him jerking his head behind us. "Let's get back to the others."

Nodding my concession, I followed him as we rejoined the formation.

We had a quick huddle as a team—there was no time for Sergio and me to confer before presenting options to the others. Our team was in this together, every opinion equally valid until one was selected as our course of action.

And yet when Sergio and I relayed news of the bridge's destruction, I found the others looking not to him, but to me.

Cancer spoke first. "So what now, Suicide?"

"What do you think?" Sergio said. "We keep following the river. Find another crossing point."

From his litter, Viggs shook his head. "I don't think we can manage that. Not with me weighing you down."

"Don't be an asshole," Reilly scolded. "Now you're just casualty-shaming yourself."

Viggs persisted, "Think about it. River's so heavily vegetated that if you take your eyes off the shore, you could miss a crossing point."

"So?"

"The curves, man. Think how coiled this river is— you're exponentially increasing the distance walked by following it, and most of that length is watched by river spotters looking for boat activity. If we don't have a specific crossing point, we'll be marching endlessly."

Sergio concluded, "Then we march endlessly."

I looked to Viggs lying helpless on the stretcher and considered the implications of what I was about to say. War held many horrors, I thought, but none worse than losing your own people. We were hunted, outcast; there was no getting out of this unscathed.

I said, "We keep following the river until we find spotters. Move in fast, hit them before they get a call out. Make them tell us the nearest crossing point."

"All right," Cancer said, "but what then? You do a thing like this, you gotta do it all the way. Otherwise you're creating more danger, not less."

I met his gaze and nodded. "One step at a time. Just worry about finding the spotters first."

Sergio ordered, "You heard the boss. Let's go."

* * *

The decision made, we continued moving, but I caught Reilly casting me disapproving glances as we rotated positions on Viggs's litter. Cancer, by contrast, looked relieved at my decision, while Sergio gave no further indication of having an opinion on the matter.

Sergio abruptly called a halt, waving us forward.

We took turns peering uphill through the brush at a ramshackle structure overlooking the river from a small hill, its faded wooden surfaces overgrown with vines.

I asked Sergio, "You sure it's a spotter shack?"

"Hundred percent. Based on size, no more than three occupants."

"Of course it's at the top of a hill," I muttered through gritted teeth. "Why not?"

Then I looked to Cancer, who was already shaking his head.

"We ain't getting this litter up that hill, if that's what you're thinking, Suicide."

"All right," I breathed. "We don't have to. We'll post him with a buddy down here. The other three of us head up, find out where a crossing point is, and come back down."

"We take four men up the hill," Sergio said flatly. "We don't know how many are up there, and we have to move fast and take them down hard, split everyone up before interrogation. Don't forget they're part of an early warning network. They'll be close to a radio, and if they manage to get a transmission out then we may as well turn your tracker back on."

"Fine," I agreed.

We quietly moved Viggs's litter into a thick swath of undergrowth. Reilly and Cancer carefully propped his back against a tree so he was sitting upright with his rifle in hand.

"As long as the coast is clear," Sergio instructed Viggs, "leave your radio on. We won't turn ours on and transmit until we're on our way back. Got it?"

Viggs looked weak, and I could tell the effort of being moved into a sitting position had been taxing for him. I felt conflicted as my eyes fell to the bloodied section of shirt covering his abdomen. Was it commander's guilt that he'd been stabbed, or survivor's guilt that he'd been stabbed while saving me? I couldn't tell.

But despite his fatigued expression, Viggs sounded lighthearted, almost chummy. "You boys are burning daylight, and I'm not getting any lighter. Hurry up and find us a crossing point. I'll be fine down here."

With that, the four of us began the journey uphill.

We swung wide around the backside of the high ground, away from the river. Our priority was stealth until we got close enough to take down the spotters, and during the hike I considered the implications of what we were about to do.

My father's last words had been an invocation to never harm innocents, sage advice I'd relayed to Cong, the young fighter who'd cut his teeth alongside me in Myanmar. But who was I to offer that kind of wisdom? Ian had referenced my assassination of Saamir—but to get to him, I'd killed an innocent myself. The victim was a Chicago high-rise maintenance worker who'd unwittingly entered the elevator with me. And I'd shot him in the head, barely giving a passing thought to the encounter—I was too focused on getting to Saamir.

But those were during the darkest days of my life. I was so far lost to my own demons that I was almost a different person altogether. Besides, after trading shots with Saamir and killing him minutes later, I'd left a female eyewitness alive and well. Screaming in terror, to be sure, but alive and well nonetheless.

Why? What sense did any of it make?

Most recently was Cetan, the cruel interrogator who I later encountered unarmed. At the time I held a knife, and could have easily killed him. He was infinitely guiltier than the maintenance worker I'd slayed in Chicago, and yet my instincts had told me to leave Cetan alive. Why?

Then I thought of what had happened between those two counterpoints, and my mind settled on Rio, on the little girl I'd shielded from Agustin's kill team, her paralyzing fear morphing to hatred once she was safe from a threat I'd brought into her home. I cried after that, had felt a desperate, tugging pang of emotion that had seemed lost to me since my first combat deployments to Afghanistan and Iraq. My encounter with the little girl marked a seismic shift within me, a change that continued to grow while in isolation in British Columbia.

What was the difference between the man in Chicago and the interrogator in Myanmar? Why did an innocent man die at my hand, while a guilty man lived?

And then the answer dawned on me, bringing with it a sweeping sense of newfound responsibility. Of power, whether I wanted it or not.

My encounters with those two men had occurred a year apart, yet I couldn't have reacted any differently. And in between them was the little girl in Rio.

The world hadn't changed, I realized. But I *had*.

The things I'd seen and done in Afghanistan and Iraq had removed any inherent belief in the sanctity of human life. Those days had shattered the idealistic young Army private I once was, had washed that patriotism away with the hardened and indifferent eye of experience. My memories of those first deployments after 9/11 were a blur of rotting human bodies juxtaposed with the patriotic, flag-waving fervor of homecoming ceremonies. I'd watched the life depart the eyes of the first man I'd ever killed and then been hailed a hero by well-wishing civilians after I got back to the States.

I'd lost my humanity in war, lost myself completely.

And when I did, it was amid the echoing cry of my countrymen chanting *thank you for your service.*

Since then I'd been fighting myself, trying to reclaim my humanity from an undertow of depression, insomnia, and posttraumatic stress that had caused more of my former teammates to kill themselves than we'd ever lost in combat. I knew what a pistol barrel tasted like in my mouth, knew what it felt like to drink myself to blackout to prevent pulling the trigger.

And bit by bit, I'd been succeeding at becoming human again. Leaving Cetan alive was proof of this—the man was unquestionably evil, had tormented me when he had control and cowered when the balance of power shifted back to me. Yet upon finding him unarmed, I'd left him alive. A year earlier I'd held the same evil in my soul that Cetan harbored; I'd shot that innocent man in Chicago with no more effort than it took to depress the trigger.

But no longer.

I didn't know what I now held in my soul, what meaning had been sifted from a thousand shifting sands of combat memories of guilt and loss. If some form of moral compass, then it was certainly skewed to the magnetic influence of reality in this dark underworld of crime and combat that I now glided through effortlessly. I still knew that Agustin and the Handler had to die for the evil they represented, and I fully intended to kill them both myself.

But I wasn't going to become them in the process.

* * *

Catching sight of the spotter shack through the trees

ahead, we halted our approach, then dropped our rucks and stashed them in the brush.

"We move in quietly," Sergio whispered. "The second we're spotted, it turns to shock and awe. Hit them hard; don't let anyone get a message out or fire a signal shot. Then we split them up for questioning."

I nodded along with the others, taking a final survey of our team. Sergio was all business, Reilly hesitant. Meanwhile, Cancer's nostrils were flaring. If he was any more excited about hitting this shack, he'd be panting like a dog.

The four of us approached in a stack with Cancer in the lead. As we closed on the cabin, I heard a noise I couldn't immediately place—a low, chuckling garble. When I finally recognized the sound, I couldn't believe what I was hearing until I saw the evidence for myself.

Behind the shack was a makeshift coop of wood and wire. I squinted into it and saw half a dozen chickens bustling around. This place was a resupply point, all right, and surely a welcome one at that. I imagined narco patrols moving to this preplanned stop on their facilitation corridors, stepping from the jungle for a hot meal complete with fresh eggs.

We crept along the left side of the shack, seeing glimpses of the river through the trees below. As we cleared the shack's front edge, Cancer broke into a sprint, and as the rest of us cut right to make entry, I saw him rifle-whipping a man who sat in an outdoor chair.

Reilly kicked the door open and stepped out of the way. I was first into the shack, cutting right toward a blur of movement.

A woman was leaping toward a radio hand mic. I grabbed her by the throat and threw her into the wall so hard the entire shack rattled. By the time she fell to the ground Sergio was upon her, slapping her in the face and speaking quickly in Spanish. Reilly took one look inside, saw there were no other occupants, and darted back out to help Cancer with the man.

This was a critical juncture—they were most likely to speak during the period of considerable shock that followed being captured. I glanced outside to see Cancer working his prostrate captive over with selective punches and kicks while Reilly bound his wrists. Seeing that they had their prisoner under control, I checked on Sergio. He was still speaking quickly, though the conversation appeared to be one-way: the woman was just shaking her head, muttering quietly between Sergio's open-handed slaps.

I began ransacking the shack's small interior.

Crude wooden cabinets were opened and their contents dumped onto the floor so I could check for false backings. Then I cut open bags of rice, searching for items hidden in the middle. As Reilly re-entered the building to help Sergio bind the woman, I struck gold with the heel of my boot—a section of floor rang with a hollow impact when I stomped on it.

Dropping to my knees, I used my knife to pry a floor-board and found a removable row of them nailed to a single panel of wood. Pulling up the panel and chucking it to the side, I peered down to see countless crates and bins of ammunition for rifles and machineguns. No guns, but all the bullets in the world—why not? There was no shortage of weapons in this area, but bullets were spent rather freely.

The ammo wasn't compatible with our US-produced weapons, and I pushed the metal bins aside to continue searching. Then I heard a displaced object clatter down in the space below.

Feeling for it in the shadows, I grasped a bricklike object and pulled it out to reveal an Iridium satellite phone with its number printed on the back. I stuffed the phone into a cargo pocket, then turned my attention back to the hole but found nothing of use.

Sergio called to me, "She's not talking."

"Go try the man."

Sergio called Reilly in to stand guard over the woman, and then I followed him outside. When I rounded the corner of the shack, what I saw stopped me in my tracks.

Cancer had blindfolded the man and cut all the clothes off his body. Blinded and naked, he stood helplessly with his hands tied behind his back. For his part, Cancer wasn't letting his ignorance of Spanish hold him back. He alternated slapping his captive across the face and belly and grabbing both sides of his head and flinging it back into the shack wall.

My mind flashed back to being in the man's position—naked, blindfolded, and being beaten in Myanmar. I heard the cadence of hands and fists pummeling a human body, the percussion of Cancer's prisoner impacting the shack wall amid the bustling cries of the chickens going crazy in their coop.

Unfazed by Cancer's violence, Sergio was already beginning to question the male captive. I approached the scene to see how in the hell this guy could resist Cancer's brutal exploitation.

Staring at the man's bruised face as he mumbled in Spanish, I didn't hear defiance in his tone. But I could clearly sense something else—helpless resignation.

Sergio looked back at me. "He says he's more scared of the cartel. Nothing we do to him can compare to what happens if he helps us."

Cancer whispered, "We need to change that, Suicide. Let me go to work."

I asked Sergio, "Are we sure they know a crossing point?"

"There's no way a spotter cell and resupply point wouldn't know."

"Cancer, you're certain you can get it from them?"

He nodded eagerly. "These fuckers are stalling because the enemy's closing in. All they have to do is delay, and we're dead. Unless we threaten them with something worse. You've seen what I can do with a cigarette—imagine me with a knife. Let me start carving up the man, and make the woman watch. She'll talk."

"Sergio?"

"You're the commander. This is the Outfit, not the military. There is no Law of Land Warfare here, no Geneva Convention. We succeed using all necessary measures. But," he intoned, his eyes stern, "I can't make the decision for you. Neither can our boys."

From behind, Reilly put a hand on my arm.

I hadn't even heard him come outside—he must have predicted what was about to occur and stepped out to intervene. "We can't kill these people, Suicide. They're not innocent but they're not armed, either." I saw the hurt in his eyes, sensed how scarring this event would be for him if we proceeded.

I'd be scarred too—what else was new? The difference was, I had enough stains on my soul. I could bear the burden of this to save Viggs. Hell, to save all of us. Reilly could resent me for the rest of his life, but he'd be alive to do so.

So would Viggs.

"Reilly," I said quietly. "This is about saving our team.

Stop thinking about right or wrong. Start thinking about Viggs."

"I am thinking of Viggs. He's not dead yet. We've got another day, maybe two, before he's in serious trouble with infection."

Sergio cut in, "We might not have that long, you understand?"

"Well you're not making it any easier on him with your plan. If you weren't making him carry the sniper rifle for Ribeiro, I could've snowed him out by now. We're carrying him anyway—"

I put up a hand and he fell silent. So did Sergio.

"Reilly," I asked, "what do you mean, 'snowed him out?'"

He shrugged. "Knock him out with Ketamine. Same as I did for you on the way back from Rio. But Sergio's leaving him in pain so he can shoot."

I put both hands on his shoulders.

"Reilly, you're a genius."

"What?"

I nodded toward the bound, naked man. "Give the Ketamine to him instead. I want him down for the count, as dead as you can make him look."

Turning to look at Cancer, I pointed to the back of the building.

"And Cancer, you beautiful evil bastard. Go grab one of those chickens."

* * *

Cancer dragged the bound woman outside by her arms. She looked down, sheer horror in her eyes at the sight beside the shack.

133

Her husband's body was sprawled on its side, naked and bruised. His limbs were askew, the exposed side of his face a swollen purple welt. He appeared for all the world to be dead, the image completed by the pool of blood in which he lay.

Before she could observe the scene for more than a second, Cancer threw her on top of the man. She cried out, and he slapped her hard. She rolled over the slick of blood, sobbing, and Cancer dropped to his knees beside her.

Out came his fighting knife, and he pressed it to her throat with such ferocity that I thought he was going to slice an artery by accident.

Sergio spoke a fast stream of Spanish, and I gasped as Cancer split the skin of her neck just enough to further bloody a blade already coated in fresh chicken blood. Then he wiped the flat surface of the blade against her cheek, leaving a wide, wet smear of scarlet.

Unable to stop myself, I opened my mouth to tell him to stop—but the woman was now speaking quickly, and Sergio looked up at me.

"The door to the shack is hollow. She says the maps are inside it."

Reilly dashed to the entrance, and I heard the sound of wood cracking as he kicked it apart.

When he ran back to us, he was shaking open large folded maps and tossing them aside until he found one depicting the area in our immediate vicinity. He spread it on the ground next to the woman.

Cancer hoisted her up onto her knees, angling the knifepoint into the base of her neck and instructing Sergio to tell her where to point.

But he didn't need to: the twin hash marks of a bridge were penciled across a curve in the river. There was a second set next to our previous crossing point, but these were marked out with an X.

Sergio muttered, "That's about one and a half klicks moving cross-country. Probably five or more if we'd followed the river." He looked up at me. "Nice work, Suicide."

I barely heard him. My eyes were darting among innocuous small dots drawn by hand across the paper, comparing their location to the hilltops that were numbered on our map.

And there it was, right between Hill 32 and Hill 39—a small, penciled dot in the low ground, just as Cancer had said.

I nodded. "We're in business."

The woman pointed at the two unobstructed lines marking the bridge, still sobbing hysterically. "*Que cartel eres chicos? Que cartel eres chicos?*"

"What was that?"

"She asked what cartel we are."

Cancer put the flat side of the blade under her chin and tilted her head up toward Sergio. "Tell her we're the Suicide Cartel."

Sergio obliged. "*El Cartel Suicida.*"

"Reilly," I said, "dose her with Ketamine. We need them unconscious as long as possible."

Cancer glowered at me. "We need to kill these fucking people, man. They know where we're going."

"They only know the bridge, and we'll make it across long before they're awake. Disable the radios. Grab any food we can take with us. I've got their only satellite phone."

"Think about this, man—"

"They live. That's final."

* * *

Cancer's displeasure was palpable as we jogged back to our rucks. He barely looked at me. His contempt didn't bother me in the least; the scene had escalated as much as I was willing to bear, the sight of two unconscious bodies left strewn in chicken blood more than enough carnage for me, given the circumstances. The satellite phone had been a major recovery. Had I missed its hiding place, we would have gained nothing from disabling their radios.

We gained less on the front of transportable food. They mostly had uncooked rice, and we didn't exactly have time to grill the chickens. In the end we spirited away some bruised pieces of fruit and stale bread.

"That's a great name for our team," Reilly said breathlessly as we hoisted our rucks on our backs. "The Suicide Cartel. It's edgy, it's tough, it's—"

"It's nonsensical," I corrected him, adjusting my ruck straps. "A cartel is an association of suppliers that maintain excessive market prices by limiting competition. We don't do—well, any of that."

"Reilly," Sergio said flatly, before looking to me. "Suicide. Shut the fuck up. Let's move."

Cancer led us back the way we'd come, the only sure path ringing this spotter post that was free of booby-traps. I turned on my radio and transmitted to Viggs.

"Tomcat Base."

"All good. Come on back."

Cancer froze, halting our small formation in place as he whirled to face me. "That wasn't Viggs."

"What do you mean, that wasn't Viggs?"

"I know his voice, that wasn't him. Besides, he'd confirm using your call sign. But he didn't call you Tomcat Actual, did he?"

136

Keeping my eyes on Cancer, I keyed my radio and spoke again.

"You were coming in broken, say again."

A pause. *"I'm clear down here. Nothing to report. You're good to come back."*

Cancer's gaze was resolute. I turned to Sergio, who was solemnly shaking his head.

Reilly offered, "He might be getting delirious down there. Guy's in a lot of pain—but yeah, we can't take any chances."

Then I transmitted, "Good copy. We'll be on our way in twenty minutes."

Turning off my radio, I took a quaking breath and said, "Cancer, get us off our back trail now. Take us somewhere you can get eyes-on with your scope."

Cancer swept off without a word, leading us to a short ridge stretching to the next hilltop. All the while, he kept casting glances downward, trying to orient himself to our starting point. Finding a patch of earth with a clear line of sight, he signaled for the rest of us to stop.

Then he crept forward with his sniper rifle until rising with impossible slowness to scan downhill through his scope. I could hear the others breathing behind me, and tried to make some sense of the situation. No feeling of impending doom knotted my gut, no flaring of the instinct that had saved my life on a whim in the past. So I watched Cancer with unwavering focus, impatiently trying to discern any indication of what he saw as he scanned the low ground.

At first I thought he'd been hit by a subsonic bullet— he fell backwards from his kneeling position, catching himself with a hand. I started to jump up and then stopped when I saw he wasn't wounded.

He looked to me for the first time since we'd left the spotters alive. His eyes were haunted.

Cancer's voice cracked as he whispered, "Hey, uh...Suicide."

I crawled forward to him, and he limply offered me his sniper rifle. I took the SR-25 from him. It felt heavy in my grip, and I scanned Cancer's face for any indication of what he wanted me to do.

But his eyes were canted downward, lips parted as he breathed shallowly.

I put the buttstock on my shoulder and rose to a knee, angling the barrel downward from the position he'd occupied. It was hard to adjust my vision to the magnified scope, which bounced a green blur of vegetation until I'd firmly steadied it in my grasp. I scanned the low ground, trying to discern where we'd hidden Viggs. How could I possibly tell? The brush looked uniformly dense from up here, and we'd hidden Viggs in the thickest patch we could find—

Then I saw him.

My God. How could we ever have left him alone down there?

The sight of him dealt a crushing blow of despair, like taking a sledgehammer to the chest. I almost dropped the rifle, then realized that everyone's eyes were upon me.

Forcing a breath to steady the scope, I had to fight the instinct to look away. I had to look so the others wouldn't have to, had to analyze this scene to spare Reilly and Sergio the sight. Even as I did so, I knew that I'd spend the rest of my life trying to forget this moment.

Viggs was strung up by his ankles, facing away. The rope suspending him descended from a tree limb. His shirt had been stripped; he wore only fatigue pants. He was unquestionably dead, and that was the only consolation I or any of us could take from the situation.

Hanging upside down, his strong arms had come to rest perpendicular to his torso, forming an inverted crucifix of death.

His body was slowly spinning on the rope, wheeling to face me. *Focus, David.* I

scanned for enemies in the surrounding bushes but was unable to see anyone else. Viggs's corpse completed its grotesque rotation, exposing his face to me.

His throat had been slashed, and a message written on his bare torso in blood. The words started on his stomach and descended, the last word spanning from shoulder to shoulder across his broad chest. A final cruel punctuation marred his face, almost washed away by the blood still trickling out of his now-porcelain body. Squinting through the scope's magnification, I struggled to read the words as his body continued its gentle revolution.

DO

YOU

SEE

OUR

REDEEMER

?

I sank to the ground, trying to compose myself. The Handler had told Hezbollah I was here, I knew. Now I knew one thing more: whether by informant or intelligence, Agustin had found out the same.

Looking to Sergio and Reilly, I shook my head. Reilly's mouth dropped open at the implication.

Cancer whispered, "We gotta hit 'em. Now."

"We can't."

"After what they did to Viggs, you son of a bitch, we'd better do something—"

"Listen to me, brother. Whatever's down there, they want us to come running. We'll be wiped out, and that's not going to help Viggs. Nothing will."

"We need to get his body."

"Even if we did, we can't take him with us."

"I don't expect you to understand, but we're not leaving him." His voice held anger, but I could see his eyes becoming glassy with tears.

I put a hand on his shoulder. "He's gone, brother. I'm sorry."

Trembling, Cancer lowered his head with a quaking intake of breath.

"Come on," I said. "Let's go find Ribeiro and get some payback."

We moved quietly down the backside of the hill, distancing ourselves from the remains of our lost teammate.

* * *

When we reached our new crossing point, we saw a crudely made but completely intact bridge stretching to the opposite shore. The bridge's long wooden planks completely shaded a series of girders propping it five feet above the water. There was no need to wait for nightfall to make the crossing; we'd easily be able to pass under the bridge completely unseen by spotters. Even the route we'd have to take was covered with tall reeds that would more than conceal us in broad daylight. The reeds were swishing with a light breeze that coasted over the river, the entire scene looking idyllic and peaceful.

But the placid surroundings seemed little more than cruel consolation under the circumstances. With what we'd just seen, this was almost too easy, a gift from the gods that we were far too anguished by Viggs's death to appreciate. Not only that, but I could detect a palpable sense of irrational disappointment that there *weren't* any enemy forces to overcome; I suspected we all would have preferred the instant gratification of combat to quietly and patiently crossing the river.

Nothing was said as we prepared to enter the river. Instead we broke into pairs to prep our equipment for the crossing, my partner dictated by Cancer pulling Sergio aside to construct their poncho raft together. He was blaming me for Viggs's death, and I was beginning to agree with him.

Looking to the water, I wondered if we'd be able to pass beneath the bridge without making poncho rafts at all. We may well have, but we fell into the activity nonetheless, almost by way of distracting ourselves from our loss.

I turned to Reilly, who was spreading his poncho on the ground, and set down my rucksack beside him. There was no security—everyone was beyond the point of caring, and I sensed that correcting this oversight would push our team to blows on the spot, making the situation even worse than it already was.

Instead Reilly and I arranged our rucks end-to-end on his poncho, drawing the waterproof fabric tight around our equipment and snapping it together. We tied the ends tight with 550 cord, then laid the bundle over my poncho, tightly rolling the seams into a cocoon-like second layer of waterproofing before lashing the ends together at the top of the bundle.

The end result was a huge green mass that would float on the surface, freeing us from the weight of our rucks so we could maneuver under the bridge. We dragged the poncho rafts in pairs into the high reeds, taking our first tentative steps into mud that was soon hidden under the surface of the river.

My boots sank deep into the mud, requiring a forceful effort to pull them out for the next step. The water was warmly refreshing after three days on the move, and we edged our way toward the bridge, moving slowly so the shifting reeds wouldn't be overly obvious against the drift of the wind.

We were submerged up to the waist by the time we slipped into the bridge's shadow and clumsily perched ourselves atop the X-frame wooden girders. Sergio was the first to sidestroke ten feet to the next set of girders, taking up a position before Cancer followed. Reilly and I pushed one poncho raft to them, then the other, before we sidestroked across ourselves.

Once we made it, Sergio and Cancer swam to the next set of girders. I looked down the length of the bridge's underbelly, seeing the equidistant X-shaped girder sequence repeating to the far shore.

Two down, fifty to go, I thought as I pushed the poncho rafts to them.

But we covered the distance quickly, falling into a rhythm without delay or complaint. By the time we reached girders that descended into reeds on the far shore, the swim had become a welcome reprieve from the constant foot movement through the jungle. It would have been an outright pleasant experience if Viggs were still with us; given his loss, the only thing I could think was that nothing this good lasted in the jungle. A restful break from patrol would surely be followed by some violent compromise.

* * *

We pulled ourselves through the reeds of the opposite bank, quickly dismantling our poncho rafts and donning rucksacks. Finding a long black leech on my shirt, I ripped it off and threw it writhing into the bushes.

The vegetation on the opposite bank stood in stark contrast to the verdant jungle we'd negotiated to reach it. Every plant here seemed to be bristling with thorns, their painful effects growing with the sloppiness of our fatigued movement. Insects had ravaged every plant surface, leaving ragged edges and countless gnawed holes amid leaves that hung in limp defeat.

After pushing into the jungle and away from any natural lines of approach to the bridge, we took a short security halt for Sergio and me to consult our map.

We were now far off our planned mission infil to the original target. Crossing the bridge placed us in difficult terrain; with the river behind us circling to the south, we were now too boxed in to evade. A jagged line of cliff ran along our eastern flank, joining with the river to form a waterfall to our southeast.

Ribeiro was to our northwest, and that was likewise the only direction we could effectively move. As a small recon team, this rendered us more vulnerable than I cared to think about. Only our ability to change direction freely had allowed us to survive this many compromises. But on this side of the bridge, the northwest frontier between river and cliff was only two kilometers wide. The enemy could read a map as well as we could, and if they occupied that flank quickly enough, they could easily drive us toward the waterfall. We barely broke through their lines with five men—now that Viggs was gone, we were all the more vulnerable.

Sergio and I quickly planned our route to Ribeiro. Between our current position and Ribeiro's hiding spot was a large, oblong section of low ground with ravines running into it from all directions.

"I don't like that dip of low ground," I whispered. "Too contained for us to risk getting trapped in."

Sergio nodded. "Flank it to the south?"

"That's what I'm thinking. Stay on the high ground, then skirt the cliff back northwest toward Ribeiro."

Sergio briefed Reilly on the route, and he took point to lead us out.

We climbed a ridge of high ground where the vegetation fell away, allowing us to look back to the river. A half-mile stretch snaked south of the bridge, completely free of crossing points; if we hadn't gotten that map from the spotters and moved straight-line distance to the bridge, we'd have been marching for days.

We staggered on, patrolling like zombies. After our first reduction in food, the stomach howled for sustenance with just as much intensity as if it had missed consecutive meals back in the real world. This desperate hunger increased—to a point. But when we continued long enough, when the body realized there was no food to be had, this instinct had lessened before largely disappearing altogether.

By now I barely even registered hunger, my stomach resigned to its fate and the most obvious sign of starvation being a pervasive fatigue. Walking up the slightest incline seemed an exhausting effort. None of us had touched what little food we'd gained from the spotters. We simply had no appetite in the wake of losing Viggs, no matter how much we needed calories. I felt a pounding dehydration headache that I was sure the others did as well. Enemy contact would have been a welcome distraction if we weren't so goddamned outnumbered at every turn.

But upon catching glimpses of the depression through the trees to our left, I was confident in our course of action. The low ground was a deep, thick mess of vegetation, perfect for hiding in but a nightmare if you got trapped there. With higher terrain to all sides and multiple ravines feeding into the depression, an enemy force could easily surround us and lay siege.

As we reached the eastern edge of the depression, I watched Reilly scan for a good place to cut northwest. Too soon and we'd enter the low ground; too late and we'd reach the cliff face.

Suddenly, Reilly went to ground.

The rest of us dropped in place, waiting for him to react to whatever he'd seen or heard. He was peering to his right, attention focused to our south. My heart was slamming now—there couldn't have been a much worse place for us to get compromised.

He waved me forward.

I cradled my rifle in the crooks of my elbows and crawled up to him. He whispered, "They're heading south. Definitely a search formation."

Pushing myself up, I peered around a tree. I saw only jungle until my eyes captured a glimpse of movement, then another—sure enough, men were moving not in file but spread out in a line. This was the slowest way to move, virtually useless unless you were on the hunt and certain your quarry was in the immediate vicinity.

They were searching all right, just as Reilly had said. And there was zero chance we weren't their target.

Looking closer, I saw that every visible man was clothed in the same tiger-stripe camouflage fatigues as the men we'd engaged in hand-to-hand combat. This was another Hezbollah element, I decided.

I looked back to Reilly and saw him flashing a weak smile as he offered, "Maybe they're hunting rabbits?"

A noise to our front caused both of us to lower ourselves. Apparently the formation hadn't completely passed us, because men with the same uniform trickled past—assaulters trailing the searchers, waiting for them to make contact and fix us in place so they could maneuver and finish us off. The end result was a T-shaped formation, highly suited for the purpose of destroying a numerically inferior force.

Easing ourselves backward, we crawled to the others.

"We can't go any further," I told Sergio and Cancer. "Hezbollah search party moving south."

Sergio asked, "How could they possibly know we're here?"

"I have no idea. But they're going to hit the waterfall within an hour, then turn back toward us and keep looking. We'll head back toward the bridge, create some distance, and then cut north."

Sergio winced. "Through that low ground?"

"We don't have a choice."

Reilly doubled us back on our trail, and we moved back the way we'd come. We were burning time, but there was no telling how far the Hezbollah formation stretched. Swinging wide gave us the best chance of passing around their flank. We could still make this work; we just had to tread carefully. Without a tracking device broadcasting our location, the four of us could practically vanish in the thick jungle.

It wasn't until we crossed the ridge of high ground

overlooking the river that I realized how much trouble we were in.

The trickle of movement on the far south bank of the river was easily discernable; I knew before Cancer put his scope to the formation that they were local cartel forces patrolling their own turf.

Squinting through his scope, Cancer said, "I count eight so far, but they're still going in and out of view. Dogs at the front, but no one's tracking yet. Making a beeline for the bridge." He lowered his sniper rifle and glared at me, whispering in a mocking tone, "Wonder how they found us."

Sadly, he was right—there was zero chance they'd effectively guessed where we were headed, short of the spotters awakening and telling them.

"We shoulda killed those spotters. Cartel has executed them both by now anyway."

Sergio asked, "How much time you think we have?"

"Quick as they're moving, they hit the bridge in an hour, max. If we're lucky, they'll have some rest breaks. But on the bridge"—he shrugged suggestively—"they'd be ducks in a row. I could probably take out half of 'em and drive the rest into the jungle."

I shook my head. "Not worth compromising ourselves —the cartel will just send more people, and Hezbollah would crush us before that. Our only safety is in hitting Ribeiro to earn repatriation, then calling the Outfit before we get overrun. At least now we know how Hezbollah beat the cartel here."

"How?"

"The Outfit is monitoring cartel radio traffic. The Handler's listening in and maneuvering Hezbollah behind the scenes."

Reilly said, "The Organization doesn't deal with terrorists."

I thought of Sasa on the hill in Somalia, asking the Handler's people to contact him, and how the Handler had immediately recognized Sasa as a sixty-five-year-old Yemeni Al Qaeda operations officer.

"I've met a high-ranking Al Qaeda guy who had direct contact with the Handler's people, who obeyed the Handler's orders. The Organization doesn't admit they deal with terrorists. At their core, they *are* terrorists." I sighed. "Believe me, the Handler is maneuvering Hezbollah behind the scenes."

Sergio commanded, "Reilly, take us into the low ground. Move fast to minimize our exposure time. I want us back on the high ground to the north as soon as possible."

And with that, we entered the depression.

As soon as we dropped into the low ground, I knew we'd been right to attempt bypassing it. Aside from the tactical nightmare of being surrounded by higher terrain in all directions, the low ground meant muddy earth that we couldn't avoid leaving tracks in, coupled with thick vegetation that hid us well but took longer to penetrate.

Reilly did the best he could to thread us through a clear route, but progress was unavoidably slow. But that was the least of my worries—I was too busy considering whether I'd recklessly endangered us by leaving the spotters alive.

Of course they were dead already, just as Cancer had said. We all saw how terrified they were of cartel repercussions for cooperating with us. What were they going to say when they woke up—that we'd done a really great job of tricking them with Ketamine and chicken blood?

Knowing full well that the spotters would eventually wake up and find a way to report, I thought we'd have *plenty* of head start over the cartel. But I'd miscalculated that too; we lost some of our advantage by having to slip under the bridge unseen, while the cartel could narrow that gap by racing across in full view of their own spotters. And I hadn't anticipated that the cartel's radio traffic would result in a nearby Hezbollah unit entering the fight.

We soon began climbing back onto the high ground without incident, clawing our way out of the swampy depression no more worse off than a few scratches and a bit of time lost. From here, we could shoot a near-straight beeline north, needing only to bypass a few clearings to reach Ribeiro's compound well before sunset. Then we could take a tactical pause and chart a hasty assault plan. This much was no small feat; we had no idea how the enemy would be arrayed on that objective, or what the exact layout of structures would be.

But escaping our immediate vicinity was infinitely better than slugging it out with the cartel and Hezbollah, and in a strange way I felt confident about our odds. We'd been on the run, fighting for our survival, and had long crossed the point of having nothing to lose. Four men in such a position, synched with one another and reacting instinctively, could do a tremendous deal of damage with the element of surprise on their side.

The air felt good on the high ground; soon we ascended a series of ridges where the breeze cooled us and the land fell away on either side, revealing a beautiful sweeping landscape we'd rarely been high enough to observe.

On point, Reilly halted abruptly.

But his body language reflected no danger; if anything, it was quite the opposite. He looked to his left, turning to make eye contact with us. Then he pointed to his ear and swung his finger to the western sky.

Then we heard it too—a helicopter.

Gradually we located the tiny approaching dot, then another identical aircraft trailing behind and to the side. Soon a third helicopter became visible, then a fourth.

"Outfit?" I whispered to Sergio.

He nodded. "Strike force. Must be the shooters they mobilized for direct action back when we had a recon objective."

The helicopters were flying in staggered pairs. They must have plotted a landing zone big enough for two at a time, and as we searched the ground to our front we saw a big enough clearing a quarter mile ahead, the high grass occupying enough space for twin aircraft landings, but just barely.

And sure enough, the first two aircraft descended into the clearing. Birds blasted out of treetops disturbed by the rotor wash as the helicopters flared to touch down. As soon as the aircraft stopped amid the whipping high grass, they disgorged their loads—tiny figures of Outfit shooters leapt out, streaming to the edges of the clearing as the helicopters lifted off.

Then the second pair of helicopters followed suit, doubling the number of Outfit operators on the ground before thundering skyward.

Cancer said, "They must've found Ribeiro's location. Perfect offset distance for a strike team to walk in."

"That's a huge force," Reilly noted. "With that many shooters, they're definitely after a high-value target."

I nodded, recalling the Handler's Chief Vicar of Defense speaking to me about the war in South America.

Before he'd known I was an assassin, he'd boasted to me about the Outfit's capabilities of finding the Handler's enemies.

...once somebody crosses the Organization, their lifespan drops to thirty days or less in most cases. If someone's really got unlimited resources at their disposal, they might make it a year. But we always get our man...

What happened next was so unexpected that for a few fleeting moments of disbelief, none of us said a word. In a way, none of us needed to: no explanation was needed, no possible theories could explain away what we were seeing.

Once the strike force was on the ground, the Outfit shooters didn't assemble to the north side of the clearing and set a quick pace in tactical formation toward Ribeiro's location.

Instead, they fanned out to the south, toward us—and the first wave spread out in a row. Behind them, the second wave fell into a front-to-back file: an assault element, waiting for the searchers to locate their quarry and fix them by gunfire. The combination was a T-shaped formation that had only one explanation.

They were hunting us.

Our only saving grace was seeing the Outfit and determining their intentions the moment they landed. We had no choice but to flee back south—proceeding toward Ribeiro would spell our interdiction by the Outfit. And whatever they'd been told, there was no negotiating with them on the ground. We'd probably been reported as rogue, perhaps even traitors who sold out to Ribeiro's side. Whatever lies had been conjured, only killing Ribeiro and announcing it publicly over satellite communications would allow us to be recovered and debriefed rather than killed in the jungle.

But with the Outfit in play, we no longer knew how to accomplish that singular goal.

We raced southward over our original tracks, moving to take refuge where no one else would: in the worst depths of the swampy depression, the only place where we could buy some time to determine our next move. Our enemies wouldn't want to enter that tangle any more than we did, and they wouldn't take the chance until they either knew we were there or had exhausted all other search possibilities.

Once we reached a suitable hiding place, we fell into our now-familiar huddle. I began, "All right, guys. We tried to outrun everyone to reach Ribeiro. Great plan, until the Outfit showed up. Now we can't proceed toward Ribeiro without annihilating ourselves." Laying the map out between us, I continued, "So let's put our heads together. There's got to be a way out of this; we just have to find it."

Sergio stroked his throat. "We've got three enemy forces surrounding us, and we've used about half our ammunition and demo. Even if we manage to break through one of the lines, we'll be overrun almost immediately."

It was maddening—so many forces arrayed against us, all set in motion by the Handler. We'd found a way out with a little help from Ian, then lost it all by the slightest possible margin. We had been on the brink of irrefutably bringing ourselves out alive, and now we'd been even further damned. Sergio was right: we were trapped inside a triangle of death. We had cartels to our southwest, Hezbollah to our southeast, and the Outfit to our north.

Reilly offered, "We can't be overrun if we leverage a

terrain feature that our pursuers aren't willing to risk. We can jump off the waterfall to our south."

Sergio squinted at the map. "Judging by the contour lines, we're looking at a hundred-foot drop."

"Could be survivable..."

"Depending on what's beneath it. Deep pool? Maybe. But if it's shallow, we're done for."

We were boxed geographically as much as tactically. The river we'd just crossed was a death trap even if cartel militia didn't block it. On the other side of our triangle, a sheer drop down the side of a cliff paralleled the axis between the Outfit and Hezbollah.

"Look at this row of cliffs, though," Cancer said, pointing to the map.

Reilly groaned. "Contour lines make that look even steeper than the waterfall."

"You're not accounting for the trees, man. That'll reduce the height to impact. We could link arms and jump. Butch Cassidy and the Sundance Kid, playa. That's the ticket."

I thought that too impossible, and yet, I couldn't come up with any better ideas. If we were to somehow bypass Hezbollah, we'd be trapped at the merger of river and cliff, their union forming the waterfall that Reilly had mentioned. I agreed with Sergio: it was too high for us to jump under all but fatal circumstances. Leaping over the cliff face would likewise be suicidal. The only way out was north, toward Ribeiro.

Then Sergio said, "We're putting the cart before the horse. Let's say we make it out of this, where do we go?"

"Argentina's non-extradition treaty," Cancer replied quickly.

"The Handler doesn't care about extradition."

And the Outfit was unquestionably the most

dangerous of our three pursuing enemies. They blocked the route north, the one way we needed to move. In a sickening twist of irony, they unknowingly occupied territory a stone's throw from their highest-value target, yet had no idea. And we couldn't tell them, because the act of doing so would result in our death.

"I'm just saying," Cancer argued, "if Nazi war criminals could hide here, so could we."

"But Paraguay's the wild west," Reilly said. "No counterterrorism laws. Very little regulation of illegal commerce. We need to get out of the jungle eventually."

The remaining terrain in our immediate vicinity appeared useless to our cause—the broad swath of low ground we were now in stretched northeast, toward a clearing at the cliff's edge that would do little but expose us.

Sergio dealt himself into the new debate. "That's exactly why Brazil is the answer."

Reilly shook his head. "You're crazy."

"We don't need the least regulation; we need the most people. It'll be easiest to hide in a densely populated area. And you're all forgetting that we'll need to find employment to sustain ourselves until we get this sorted out."

"Legal employment? Not a chance."

"I never said legal—"

Cancer interjected, "And what's to sort out? We can't ever go back now. Hitting Ribeiro was our last hope."

"We'll figure it out."

"We will? Who, exactly? You? Me? Suicide?"

Reilly offered, "For now, we just need some time and distance. Maybe we could hide for now, let our enemy leave, then hit Ribeiro later."

My mind was swimming. I'd spent so much of my

adult life trying to seek combat and adrenaline; now I was up to my neck in it with no way out.

And I had three lives to save.

I vaguely heard Cancer talking. "Think we're gonna hide with all these people swarming around here? Someone's coming in this swamp, if they don't find us elsewhere. Besides, you heard those helicopters. Ribeiro will be gone the second things quiet down. So what'll it be, boss?"

"Yeah," I said, looking up from the map.

They waited for me to say something, saw that my mind was elsewhere. Then Sergio addressed me directly, his eyes on mine.

"David," he said quietly, "what do you want us to do?"

WILLPOWER

Ira deorum

Wrath of the gods

9

I looked back to the map, studying the terrain as if it held some answer. It had to; everything we discussed was insignificant if we couldn't leverage the terrain to our advantage.

Almost everything else, I corrected myself. The arrangement of enemy forces played no small role in all this, though they were more of a package deal. We were surrounded, plain and simple.

I thought back to our first mission compromise, when the tracking teams and dogs had descended upon us. My reaction had proved right: a one-man ambush assuming all risk so the others could flee to safety.

But in this case, the enemy numbers were too many. I wouldn't defeat any more than the lead scouts this time, not even close. Was there any way I could make defeating the lead scouts enough, as I had before? I scanned the map—the contour lines, the river and waterfall, the cliff and Ribeiro's location. Considering the enemy's current formation, with us in the center, I felt the solution beginning to come to me.

"We're still going to hit Ribeiro," I announced. My eyes

focused on the depression where we were now located. On first glance it appeared of no use to us beyond a hiding spot, but this swamp was the key to both Ribeiro's death and our survival.

Everyone stared at me as I continued, "We could theoretically break the lines; it just won't do any good because we'll get smashed shortly thereafter. Right?"

Sergio grunted. "No question."

"And we've got three forces against us. The cartel is using dogs and trackers. Hezbollah's being fed reports from the Handler based off our transmissions. And the Outfit's not only got access to any information we transmit, they also have the means to geo-locate our tracker. Agreed?"

Cancer nodded. "Geo-location is probably one of the main reasons they're on the ground. Jungle canopy usually blocks the signal from the air. But the Outfit will have ground equipment that will see it light up like a Christmas tree. So what?"

"The Handler isn't going to fling that huge Outfit strike force against the cartel or Hezbollah. My guess is we've been on the run for three days with rolling contact, and the Handler is getting impatient. So Plan A is cartel kills us; Plan B is Hezbollah kills us. And the Outfit is Plan C, staging to see if our tracker begins evading north so they can kill us if the first two plans fail. Right?"

Sergio replied, "Probably."

"I'll bet no one knows about Hezbollah except the Handler and some of his top people—the Organization doesn't officially deal with terrorists, right? No one's controlling the cartel, just monitoring their transmissions to figure out where we're at. And the Handler has a direct line of control with the Outfit."

Cancer asked, "There a point to this?"

I waved a hand dismissively. "At the highest levels, someone knows where all these elements are. But on the ground, no single element has the entire picture."

Reilly said, "Sure, except for us. Now that we've, you know, barely avoided a gunfight with each of the three enemy forces in the past few hours."

Inhaling deeply, I replied, "Well, that ends now."

"Which element are you proposing we engage?"

"All of them. At once."

Sergio interjected, "What do you have in mind?" His tone indicated I'd better have some profound point following on the heels of this declaration. Cancer and Reilly were watching me impatiently.

I continued, "Right now, the Handler is the puppeteer behind this little spectacle of horror. So we take control of the strings. Shake up the situation on the ground. Set a chain reaction of events so when each unit responds, it's beyond the Handler's ability to control it. And if they're all fighting each other, they're not fighting us. We can slip out in the fray—without being pursued—and hit Ribeiro."

Sergio replied, "We'll be able to fool the cartel and Hezbollah, potentially. Make them do what we want. But the Outfit isn't going to blindly run into a trap."

"That's why we make it look like we're still good company men. Remember, the Outfit isn't a hundred percent certain that we know they're out to kill us. So we radio in, report we've got a casualty and cannot proceed. I'll activate the tracker right here. Sergio, what does that trigger?"

He thought for a moment. "Outfit will pick up the signal, relay the tracker grid to higher. They'll be ordered to set up a picket line in case we break north." He looked at the map, pointing to an east-west running ridge. "Probably on this high ground. That's where I'd set up."

"And then?"

"Then the Handler passes our tracker grid to Hezbollah so they can kill us."

"So that's step one—get the Outfit to set up a barricade, prepared to follow the tracker if it comes to them. But it won't. It'll stay right here, so they'll remain in position."

"Then what?" Reilly asked.

"I propose we split into pairs. One pair stays here in ambush to wait for Hezbollah's arrival. The other heads west, toward the cartel. This pair gets as close as they can to the cartel but doesn't engage until they hear the other pair trading shots with Hezbollah."

"Okay," Sergio allowed. "So one pair is engaging Hezbollah, and the other pair is engaging the cartel."

"Then both teams do the same thing: we smoke a few dudes, piss off the bad guys, and then haul ass straight toward the center of the Outfit line. Once the cartel and Hezbollah are pursuing the two halves of our team, they're not stopping to make radio communications with anyone."

Sergio nodded. "So the Handler goes from having control of three elements to only having control of the Outfit."

"And the Outfit is staged," I continued, "exactly where we want them. Why should they move? Their orders are to monitor the tracker, remain out of the fight unless we evade north toward them. They're hearing some sporadic gunfire to their south—no wonder, because they see our tracker standing still. Every indication points to us getting overrun right here, where we called in and where our tracker is still broadcasting."

"And meanwhile," Cancer said ominously, "we're

bringing every bad guy this side of the river running straight into the Outfit."

I nodded. "Outfit's on the high ground. We get into the low ground in front of them, try to meet up and hide until the cartel and Hezbollah converge. That's going to be a massive three-way gunfight. Then we run the gap, one way or the other—between the Outfit and cartel, or between the Outfit and Hezbollah, depending on how the situation unfolds. Either way, we flank around the Outfit while they're gainfully employed fighting off everyone that's trying to hunt us. Then we blast north toward Ribeiro."

Sergio muttered, "*Santa mierda*, Suicide. That's genius."

Reilly looked to Sergio. "You going to let this slide?"

"Let what slide? It sounds like our only choice."

Reilly explained, "We should send the Outfit to a false grid, get them moving in another direction. Not leave them in the fray with these assholes from the cartel and Hezbollah. I don't want to risk losing one of our boys."

"They're not 'our boys' any longer," Sergio corrected. "It's just us now—and we can't afford not to bring the Outfit into play."

Cancer added, "You want us to get smoked so the Outfit doesn't risk getting cut? They're trying to kill us, man."

"It's the orders that are fucked," Reilly protested, "not our people. They're not ordering themselves: it's the Handler."

I began, "Be that as it may—"

Reilly cut me off. "It may, Suicide. Let's not mince words."

"Fine. I'd love to avoid exposing Outfit shooters to danger, but Cancer's right." I shot him a disapproving glare and added, "For once." Then I looked back to Reilly. "We won't have any brothers in the Outfit until we repatriate. And we don't stand a chance of repatriation unless we pull off this plan and deliver Ribeiro's head on ice. We've got enough risks as it is. I'm not increasing the danger to us in any way that I can avoid."

"This decision is going to come out in the wash," Reilly said. "How's our chance of repatriating when they find out we put Outfit shooters in mortal danger?"

My hands tightened into fists and my heart fluttered as I spoke in a low voice. "That decision and the consequences are mine. I'll take full responsibility once we make it out—but we've got to get there first."

Reilly shot back, "You left those spotters alive. Why are you willing to get Outfit people killed?"

"The spotters weren't a matter of life or death for my men. This is."

Cancer interjected, "They were a matter of life or death for Viggs."

I closed my eyes for a beat, feeling my jaw flex. Letting the comment wash over me, I continued, "My job is to keep you three alive. All other loyalties are secondary to that. So this is decided."

Sergio spoke at once. "Task organization, gentlemen. Based on what we've seen, Hezbollah will move quicker than the cartel. I dare say that Suicide and Cancer are the faster runners among us—so you two stay here on Hezbollah duty."

Cancer's face was twisted in resentment; he didn't bother trying to conceal his displeasure. I waited for him to object, to do his part in breaking this arrangement. But he said nothing, and that told me all I needed to know.

I began, "But—"

"And since the cartel is slower," Sergio continued,

"Reilly and I will move out to locate them. As soon as possible after hearing you and Cancer invoking the wrath of the Muslim hordes, we'll open fire on the cartel."

"I'm not sure if—"

"Then the four of us do our best to link up in the low ground to the north, short of the Outfit's position. If that's not possible, our rally point is here." He pointed to a small clearing well north of where we'd seen the Outfit land. "Eastern tip of this clearing. Whoever arrives first, wait thirty minutes for linkup. If no one else shows, continue mission. Kill Ribeiro, contact the Outfit, and repatriate. Questions?"

I was already pulling the tracker out of my kit and turning it on.

It came to life with a miniscule red light.

"Just one question," I said.

"Tracker's on?"

"Yeah, but—"

"Accounting for the Outfit picking it up and relaying to higher, I'd say Hezbollah will be on the way within ten minutes."

"Probably, yeah."

"You had a question, Suicide?"

"Not to contradict you, Sergio," I began, "but the odds of Cancer shooting me are as high—or higher—than him helping me kill any enemy. This is a perfect opportunity for him to smoke me without consequence." I met Cancer's eyes. "No offense."

Cancer held my stare and gave me a slow smile.

Sergio didn't budge. Instead he looked to Cancer and asked softly, as if speaking to a child, "Cancer, if I leave you alone with Suicide, can you restrain yourself from fragging him?"

"Nope."

Sergio closed his eyes and nodded. "Just...do your best." His eyes opened and flicked to me. "Suicide, make the call. We don't have any more time to spare."

* * *

"Halo One, Halo One," I gasped, panting for breath. "This is Tomcat Actual."

I received an immediate response this time. Who would have guessed?

"Tomcat Actual, this is Halo One. Send your traffic."

"Be advised, Tomcat element under pursuit," I said, panic in my voice. "We have wounded, cannot proceed. Mission abort, mission abort! Request emergency recovery, stand by for grid."

"Go ahead."

I transmitted our grid, and then added, "You better send a rescue quick, or it might be too late."

"Halo One copies all. Remain at your current location, over."

I replied disjointedly, flickering the transmit button on my hand mic to produce the effect of a broken transmission.

"Advise ETA... rescue... medic for... copy, over?"

"You're coming in broken. Say again."

"Request... transport... litter for... Tomcat..."

Releasing the transmit button, I turned off my radio and set the mic down.

Then I collapsed my satellite antenna and looked to Sergio. "How was that for fucked-up new team leader?"

Cancer cut in, "Pretty convincing. Then again, you've had a lot of practice."

"Cancer," Sergio scolded, "play nice, goddamnit. Reilly and I are out of here. We'll do our best to hold off engagement until we hear you two shooting. If we don't see you in the low ground, we'll meet up at the rally point. Eastern tip of that clearing. Remember, if no one's there, wait thirty minutes and continue mission. No matter what."

He held up a fist, knuckles outward, and everyone took turns pounding it with their own.

"Good luck," Reilly said. "See you boys in the low ground."

Then the two of them departed, leaving me and Cancer alone.

Cancer raised an eyebrow toward me. "Problem?"

* * *

Cancer and I set up our ambush less than twenty meters offset from the tracker, which we'd left in place. Our goal wasn't to watch the tracker but to stand guard over Hezbollah's approach route. Hitting them at a distance gave us the best possible chance of escaping to the north.

And there we stayed, lying next to one another, one boot each touching at the point of a V-shape, our torsos angled outward so we collectively watched a 180-degree swath of jungle to the south.

Cancer was quiet for a long time before whispering, "You're really afraid I'll kill you out here, aren't you?"

"What? I, ah—" I cleared my throat. "A little bit. Yeah."

"Suicide, no offense to your delicate officer sensibilities, but if I wanted to kill you?" He gave a short laugh. "You'd be fucking dead, ten times over."

I released a silent gasp of relief but wasn't yet willing to relax.

Then, he corrected himself. "I mean, yeah, I *want* to kill you. But if I were going to—then, you'd be dead."

My breath caught in my throat. "I may not be God's

gift to the death squad, but what's your beef? Yes, I'm responsible for leaving Viggs alone. But it wouldn't have made a difference if I had been there, or you, or all of us —we'd all be dead instead of sitting here across the river."

"It ain't about Viggs. I just don't think you got what it takes, that's all."

"Even though four of us are still alive?"

"Sergio's told you. This ain't the military. It's the Outfit. No Geneva Convention here. Look at who makes it, and who doesn't. Know why I was put on cigarette duty during your Outfit selection?"

"Because you're a heavy smoker?"

"Not a lot of our guys can handle that spot, man. But I can toast a dude with cigarettes—I mean a dude with a military background, war hero or whatever. Then order him tossed in the river for good if he talks."

I said, "You're a real asshole, Cancer."

"Yeah, I am. But it ain't because I don't know where they been. I seen more war than most before I came here. But the Outfit is better, you get me? They care about results, not morals."

"So you don't feel anything, is that it?"

"Naw, I *feel* plenty. When I'm fighting or I'm killing, I'm on top of the world."

"And otherwise, you're numb."

He considered the statement. "Yeah, I never thought about it like that. But yeah. I'm numb."

"Cancer, for the first time in our relationship, I'm starting to agree with you."

"Now answer me somethin' else."

I sighed. "For you, Cancer, anything."

"You've been so close to the Handler, right? Met him so many times?"

"Yeah. I don't know how to describe him. I guess he's—"

"I don't give a flying fuck what he's like. Why haven't you killed him yet? You're a sharp little needledick, why couldn't you get it done?"

My mind swirled with a litany of past events. Infiltrating the Outfit. Killing Jais—for his betrayal, yes, but mostly to claim his meeting with the Handler. Smuggling a weapon back from Rio, bringing it within striking distance only to find Ian a hostage. Indebting myself to a deep cover operation with a golden opportunity to kill the Handler alongside Sage—only to find that my assassin mentor represented a somehow worse evil. Negotiating my return to the Mist Palace in exchange for my current assignment, which, against all odds, turned out to be worse than I could've imagined.

"It's complicated," I offered.

"Complicated my white Irish ass. *Life* is complicated. Now, is it possible?"

"Is what possible?"

"Killing him."

"God," I gasped before consciously considering the question, "I hope so." Then I gave him a curious look. "Why do you want this so bad? I thought you started hunting him for sport, because you were bored with retirement."

"Well, after Viggs, it's personal."

"Agustin killed Viggs. Whether he was there or not, he ordered it."

"Yeah, but we wouldn't be in this shit spot if the Handler hadn't dumped us here to die. You get me?"

"Yeah. Yeah, I do."

"Good. Now use your head, man. Can the Handler be poisoned?"

Sage's answer to that same question sprang through my mind: constant bodyguard accompaniment, state-of-the-art medical supplies, a doctor on standby, screening sensors that would detect anything we could obtain—except for the one serum I'd used on Sage.

"Been there, done that," I said. "Poison's a dead end."

"Explosives, then."

I rolled my eyes, even though I'd proposed the same solution in recent memory.

"Too many security screenings," I dismissed him. "Advanced sensors. Technology...whatever. It's not going to work that way."

"Then how?"

I briefly considered the red pipes on his office ceiling. I'd assumed they were a fire containment system, though Sage had assured me of the opposite. At the touch of an eight-digit code known only to a personal bodyguard and the Handler himself, he—and his office—would be incinerated. He'd built a safe room around himself and his most sensitive information in the event of outside attack, but if Sage couldn't find a way to hack or otherwise defeat it, then neither could I.

"Cancer, if I knew the answer, he'd be dead already. Okay?"

He lowered his voice to a conspiratorial tone. "People get complacent when they think they're alone. Where does he go by himself?"

This question, too, had a built-in Sage response, though for some reason this still seemed to me the most tantalizing of all available possibilities.

My thoughts drifted to the garden, the fortress within a fortress. Fifteen-foot wall topped with barbed wire ringing a personal sanctuary where the Handler had staged his presentation of Ian's capture. It was the only place I knew the Handler or his daughter to ever tread alone, and yet Sage had dismissed even this by virtue of fence and perimeter guard.

I began, "There's one place he's alone. But we can't hit him there."

"Because?"

"Because—"

My response was halted by the sound of grenades detonating to the west. We both fell quiet to listen, and before long, the explosions faded to the chatter of automatic weapons returning fire.

Cancer whispered, "That's Sergio and Reilly breaking contact. Cartel's inbound to the Outfit, and no Hezbollah in sight. What you gonna do now, Suicide?"

"We've got to move north now, shoot the gap while we can."

"Wrong."

"Wrong?"

"Pro tip number one: always side with raw aggression. We move south, find Hezbollah, and punch 'em in the throat. Then *didi mao* toward the Outfit."

"We'll lose time heading the wrong way. And by the time we find Hezbollah and turn around, they'll be on our asses."

"So we run faster. And David?"

"Yeah?"

"Pro tip number two: don't be a pussy."

Ending his sermon on that particular note of wisdom, Cancer was on his feet and moving forward.

I wanted to order him back, furious that he'd made a snap decision without approval and executed it on his own. Then I remembered how many times I'd done the exact same thing, if not outright violated a direct order.

Now my own karma was coming back to haunt me.

Pushing myself up, I followed him and advanced into the jungle to our south, toward Hezbollah.

* * *

I was certain we wouldn't have to move for long to find our enemy; after all, our tracker had been activated for no small amount of time, and Hezbollah couldn't be far.

But as we advanced quickly and quietly twenty meters to the south, then fifty, I felt panic sink in. By now there was no gunfire to our west; the cartel was headed toward the Outfit full bore, with Sergio and Reilly leading the charge.

Enough, I thought. I was going to order us to turn back and take our chances—the Outfit was well-armed, and we had to attempt our flanking maneuver while they were engaged. If the cartel gunfight had started and ended before our arrival, then Cancer and I were as good as dead.

No sooner had I made my decision than Cancer stopped behind a tree, as if to catch his breath. I caught up and grabbed his arm, but he flung my hand away and raised his SR-25 instead.

I scanned the jungle to our front, seeing nothing but a gulley rolling into high ground on the other side.

Tick.

That's how quiet the subsonic shot was—slightly louder was the sound of Cancer's bolt cycling, but I still could've convinced myself I was hearing things. Until the scalding hot shell casing from his round hit me in the neck and flew inside my collar, tumbling between my bare chest and shirt.

I hissed in pain, pulling at the bottom of my shirt to let the casing fall out, just as the world erupted into gunfire.

Cancer and I hit the ground, shocked by the shots' proximity. It seemed as if we'd run into a row of soldiers spread on-line to face us—because, I realized, we *had*.

By some twist of fate, the lead element of the T-shaped search-and-destroy formation was in the low ground just ahead of us. Cancer had taken a shot at what he thought was the leading edge, but it had actually been a trailing element briefly visible through the trees.

I poured a magazine's worth of automatic fire into the low ground as Cancer hucked in two grenades to buy us time.

My rifle went empty between his twin grenade explosions, and then our race began.

We hadn't bought ourselves much time; the Hezbollah fighters recovered and gave chase much quicker than I'd hoped. Sergio had chosen Cancer and me for this role because we were the two fastest, but the enemy behind us was faster.

Cancer and I zigzagged between trees as I struggled to reload my rifle. We were running hard now, as fast as our surroundings permitted, and I still wasn't sure it would be enough. The forest around us whipped by in streaks of green, leaves slapping our faces and branches clawing at our clothes and equipment as if to drag us to the jungle floor. Bullets tore through the brush. The air was filled with the alternating cracks of bullets accelerating through the sound barrier and then decelerating to a stop in tree trunks.

I could hear men running behind me, fragments of shouted commands. They were gaining ground—we had to run patterns so they'd miss, but they could track us in straight-line distance because they were the ones shooting.

If I stopped to shoot back, I'd be dead before I raised my rifle.

Instead I fumbled in my pouches with one hand and, finding a grenade, pulled the pin and tossed it over my shoulder without looking. It detonated within ten steps, sending a rolling shockwave of noise and debris over my back.

That should do it, I thought—but our pursuers continued closing in. These guys were tough, but so was grenade shrapnel. I repeated the process, tossing a second frag behind me. This explosion seemed to do little more than alter the direction of pursuit as men charged after me, fearlessly bounding past anyone killed or injured in the blast.

When it seemed like the hail of gunfire slicing through the jungle couldn't get any more intense, I found a third grenade and yanked the pin.

Then I dropped it in place.

The dense metal sphere bounced off my boot as I accelerated, trying to outrun the blast radius. Two steps beyond, then three, before I kicked a tree root and stumbled. My mind processed three words—*that's not good*, an oddly understated response in place of any combination of profanity more suited to such a transgression.

Recovering my stride, I poured every last drop of speed possible into my final steps before the blast. My mind recounted minimum safe distances, ranges the fragments could fly, as I desperately tried to latch onto the tree density around me as a means for survival.

But tree cover or not, when the blast occurred, it knocked me down.

I flipped over my own feet, shoulder blade clipping a tree and bringing me to a painful stop. My head was ringing, a muddy cloud of earth whipping across me.

Knocked so off-kilter that I couldn't tell which way I needed to run, I tried to blink my vision clear. Everything was smoke and dust around me, making it impossible to orient myself.

Wasting valuable seconds, I consulted my compass and watched the needle wobble to the north. Then I hauled myself upward and clumsily ran, my shoulders knocking off trees amid the reduced visibility.

Gradually I cleared the dust cloud and picked up my pace. It was too late—even through ringing ears I could make out the sounds of pursuit, additional men who'd raced clean through the grenade explosion, unencumbered. Christ, how many people did they have?

More gunshots behind me, closer than I cared to estimate, forcing me to run a zigzag pattern again. But I felt too slow, too encumbered by trying to negotiate a way between the trees. Too messed up from the grenade blast, and no time to recover my bearings. They'd be upon me in ten seconds.

Reaching into my kit for another grenade, I instead discovered that all the pouches were now empty.

I patted my kit frantically as I moved, searching for just one more frag but finding none.

Between disorientation and my panicked search, I took my eyes off the path ahead. My boot caught something—root, vine, what did it matter—and I tumbled headlong into the dirt.

Men were almost atop me now, and I rolled onto my back. I raised my M4 to see four Hezbollah fighters in tiger-stripe camouflage skidding to a halt, amazed at their luck.

This was it, I thought as I took panicked aim at the lead man. I was dead, but I was taking as many of these motherfuckers with me as I could.

After that, everything was frozen in time. I clacked off two rounds at the lead man, a seeming eternity between my shots. He looked almost peaceful, as if relieved that he'd stopped running. A puff of fabric on his shirtfront as the first round struck, his expression unchanged when the second bullet ripped through his jaw.

Before he began to fall forward, I observed the other three men as if they were moving underwater, my mind processing their actions at a fantastic rate. I could see the angles of their AK-47s, my own aim shifting without any conscious direction to the man who'd be first to shoot me.

I felt the thump of the buttstock against my shoulder, a bullet casing ejecting sideways out of my weapon. By the time I pulled the trigger again he was gut shot from my first round—good enough.

My mind cycled seamlessly; my thoughts were acute, my body totally free of pain. Two enemies left unharmed, one's rifle slightly more angled toward me than the other's. Too late, I knew even as I swung my aim to him. Better hope he misses, David, because you're not beating him to the draw. My mind had time to process all of this and more. Then his head recoiled with a jolt.

Skull fragments and brain matter arced outward in slow motion. I gave no thought to who'd shot him or why, simply shifted my rifle to the man beside him. No time to take aim before his head, too, caught a bullet that ripped into his forehead and ejected much of his brain matter. The entire scene had a surreal, music-video quality, and as both enemies tipped forward like felled trees, a man's shout brought me back to reality.

"GO!"

Cancer, behind me. "GO! GO!"

Time compressed to an impossibly fast rate—in a fraction of a second all four bodies were crashing to the earth, and I was in the present moment. On my back, alive, with an army bearing down upon me.

Rolling to my side, I launched up and outward in a stumbling run toward the sound of Cancer's voice. I couldn't see him, could only hear men crashing through the brush toward their dead friends. Then the *tick, tick* of Cancer's SR-25 throwing subsonic rounds into the jungle. I had to be practically on top of him to hear it, though it took me an additional moment to locate him atop a small ridge to my front.

He'd made it out of the depression, and I scrambled up the rise toward him, my boots slipping against the soft earth.

Cancer planted a hand on the back of my shirt and awkwardly hoisted me up, giving me enough of a boost to fall over the edge.

"Come on," he breathed, and then he was gone—running again, moving north.

I followed him as fast as I could manage, gaining ground until we were almost side-by-side, threading our way through the jungle. Suddenly a massive wave of gunfire broke out, but not at us—this was off to our west. The cartel had collided with the Outfit's line, opening up the first flank of a battle we'd have to outrun.

Tree cover began to thin as Cancer and I closed on a jagged ravine, one of the many leading into the depression. Cancer vaulted it first and I followed a split-second behind him, continuing to run on the other side.

Then a strange wall of dirt rose in a wave, spreading left to right—a burst of machinegun fire impacting a few meters ahead.

Its source was on the high ground to our front, and we scrambled back the way we'd come just as sporadic rifle fire joined the machinegun.

Reversing direction revealed the scattered movement of Hezbollah fighters approaching us, sliding their way forward between the trees.

Without looking to see how deep it was, Cancer and I flung ourselves into the ravine.

We rolled fifteen feet down a muddy slope, boots stopping in spongy earth soaked by water. Then we began to run east, with him in the lead.

We raced down the ravine, caught in the center of a storm as the Outfit and Hezbollah elements clashed around us. Automatic fire zipped overhead; soon I could hear men crashing into the ravine far behind us. To what side they belonged, I couldn't tell.

We plunged headlong down the ravine, hoping against hope that we'd outrun the massive collision of men around us.

Beyond the slamming of my heart and my ragged gasps for air, the outer world turned to chaos. Three sides fighting one another, the gunfire joined by the low explosions of grenade rounds detonating. How many Outfit guys would die in this? Whatever the number, I'd have to answer for them all—but I had to survive it first.

The ravine dipped into the low ground, then crested up a hill as we outran the sounds of battle. Cancer darted into the sunlight, sliding to a halt so suddenly that I crashed into him.

He hissed with fear, and I saw why as we skidded forward three feet to a stop at the edge of the dirt.

The ground beyond his feet fell away in a wall of rock that descended eighty feet to a blanket of treetops. To our front was crystal blue sky, hazy streaks of white cloud spread above an idyllic view of endless jungle.

I grabbed his shirt and pulled him backward. He turned to glare at me for running into him, his face devoid of its usual color. Eyes furious, burning into me. I gave an embarrassed shrug.

Without a word, we clambered over the ledge to our left, pulling ourselves into the vegetation. Then we started threading our way north as the sounds of battle fell away to our left.

At one point Cancer looked in that direction, pivoting to raise his sniper rifle.

I looked to see Outfit shooters moving fifty meters away, repositioning themselves amid the rolling battle with cartel and Hezbollah forces.

Looking back to Cancer, I saw him not appraising the situation but taking aim, and so I reached out and pushed his weapon downward.

"Knock it off," I said, scolding him like a middle school teacher addressing a problem student. He shot me an irritable glance and then continued moving north.

He'd wanted to light up his own Outfit members, and would have if I hadn't been there to stop him. For a moment I felt certain that if we'd come across his entire extended family posing for a group portrait, I still would have had to physically intervene to keep him from shooting. Cancer was almost beyond control. He seemed gripped by a feeding frenzy of killing, one that he wasn't keen on stopping if he could avoid it.

* * *

We slowed as we reached our rally point, not wishing to surprise Sergio and Reilly and be mistaken for the enemy.

If they were even alive. That much remained to be seen, and my doubt began to grow as Cancer and I reached the eastern tip of the appointed clearing. After our jaunt to find Hezbollah, those two should have been far ahead of us in reaching the rally point.

But Sergio and Reilly were nowhere to be found, nor was any indication that they'd been there. We remained in the trees, performing a short patrol around the clearing to make our presence known. I listened sharply as the whistling cadence of birds and insects rose and fell, hoping to hear a whispered call from our teammates that never came.

They simply weren't there.

"What do you think?" I whispered to Cancer. "They should have been here before us. Should we continue north?"

"The plan was to wait thirty. So we need to wait thirty. Who knows what happened back there."

I nodded, and we located a spot to hide and listen for our teammates' approach. After we settled into a security position, I slid close to Cancer and whispered, "Any chance Sergio and Reilly waited half an hour and left already?"

"We were late, but not *that* late. They would've heard our approach within the time window."

Analyzing his tone and the cadence of his words, I tried to discern what he thought of their prospects without asking outright. But his voice betrayed no emotion whatsoever.

Rather than project my insecurity, I changed the subject. "What kind of enemy forces do you think we'll see at Ribeiro's location?"

He remained quiet, though whether irritated or thoughtful, I couldn't tell.

Finally he said, "There won't be many people there."

"I'm serious."

"So am I."

I was taken aback. Short of finding out what happened to Sergio and Reilly, the biggest question on my mind was how we could possibly overwhelm Ribeiro's security forces with just two—or even four—shooters.

I probed further. "How do you figure there won't be a lot of enemies?"

He ignored my question and instead asked his own.

"Suicide, why'd they kill Viggs like they did?"

I swallowed, watching a dark millipede clatter across a branch. "Obviously Viggs didn't talk. They knew they couldn't sound convincing enough on the radio to lure us back."

"And?"

"Since we'd be suspicious of any radio traffic, they staged a horrific scene to try and lure us into an ambush."

He clicked his tongue. I glanced around to see him shaking his head.

"You're missing the point," he said.

"I don't think I am."

"You're missing the fucking point. *Obviously* they tried to tempt us into an ambush, yeah. But why?"

"Why? Because they couldn't sound convincing enough on the radio—"

"Use your head. Christ, you sound dumber than Viggs right now. I ain't contesting the ambush attempt. But why not hunt us down?"

I was quiet for a while after that. When he saw I wasn't responding, he pressed on.

"I mean, this whole time we've had an infinite number of enemies on our tail. But where they killed Viggs was the easiest place to slice and dice us: they would've known without a doubt we'd gone to the spotter shack. You could practically see it from where we stashed Viggs. Not to mention all the racket we made between slappin' around those fucks and the chickens going apeshit."

I felt on the brink of understanding something vital, but I wasn't quite there. "Keep talking."

"With a little patience to move into position, they could've easily overrun us. Right? Hill didn't take that long to sneak up. But they didn't. What'd they do instead?"

I found myself nodding. "They tried to make us come to them. A gamble, under the best of circumstances."

"Game, set, match. Why restrict themselves to setting a bear trap when everyone else we've faced would've smashed us where we stood?"

Why indeed—that was the million-dollar question. My mind was speeding, darting from memory to memory in a failed bid to draw a conclusion.

Until it did.

"Cancer, you're a real asshole."

"Why's that?"

"Because you're right."

He scoffed. "'Course I am. Come on, you're the college boy. You went to the Naval Academy, not me."

"West Point."

"Whateva. So why'd they do that?"

I swallowed. "Because they didn't have the manpower to overrun us."

"Oh no? You were certain that message came from your pal Agustin. So fucking certain."

"It did. Without a doubt."

"Well he's working for Ribeiro, isn't he? How does the biggest swinging dick on the continent not have the manpower to pluck us off the face of the earth? Every terrorist pick-up team in this shithole has an army, why not Ribeiro?"

"Hezbollah's a touch more sophisticated than a pickup team, but I get your point. And I don't know how Agustin wouldn't wield the manpower—I honestly don't. But I can't think of a single other explanation for why we're alive right now."

"Me neither," Cancer admitted.

Silence settled between us. A comfortable silence, for the first time since I'd left the spotters alive. I didn't know what to say to him, but this no longer distressed me. His point was valid, prophetic even—a conclusion I'd expect a nerdy analyst like Ian to draw, not the battle-hardened sociopath beside me.

I felt a lump forming in my throat and swallowed dryly. "Do you think Ribeiro will still be in his compound?"

"That's what I can't figure out. What Ian told you, that's perishable information no matter what. What if Ribeiro could hear the choppers coming in? Or the gunfight? What about some informant sending word about the cartel and Hezbollah shooting it out?"

The murmured clicking of some frog or bug crackled at us from the undergrowth. I waited for it to go silent, then answered, "Ribeiro's options would be limited. The Handler has chipped away so much of his network, he'd practically be on the run with the clothes on his back. Right?"

"We better hope so. Whatever makes him take his chances waiting it out where he's at. Because ask yourself this, Suicide: what if he's gone when we arrive? What's our repatriation ticket then?"

I paused, gauging by the silence that Cancer hadn't intended the question to be rhetorical. Where was the line between me trying to sound optimistic as a leader and outright dishonesty?

Finally I answered, "We don't have one."

"Exactly. Now I don't know what the right answer is, but remember that whole conversation about fleeing further into Argentina or crossing the border into Paraguay? Or making a run into Brazil? That entire 'we're fucked' line of dialogue before you had your great idea about starting a battle and fleeing in the chaos? Well I'm here to tell you, buddy, you better keep that in the back of your mind. Because in a few hours we'll know if our golden goose has flown the coop or not. And if he has, you better be prepared to make some tough decisions on what we do next."

My gaze drifted to the tree beside me. Its craggy surface was covered in fibrous moss glistening with moisture whose sinews extended in a thousand directions. Then I peered into the forest beyond, trying to pull security but instead ruminating on the countless interwoven layers of plant life, all communing into a single landscape that extended endlessly.

We'd been running through that forest, fleeing death, for days now. At my core I knew we could continue running endlessly. It wasn't vanity that made me know this to be true; left on my own, I'd be lucky to make it a week.

But these men were another matter: unbeatable, unable to be vanquished by nature or man. They were made of something different than me, something better. They followed me because organizational protocol decreed me to be in charge, not because I was better at any of the myriad tasks they were capable of. Given a lifetime to train, I'd be lucky to match their abilities in a single narrow vector, much less exceed it in multiple.

But by recognizing and accepting that these men were apart from me, were better than me, I could lead them. I could understand my shortcomings and their strengths, and manage their efforts with humility and pragmatism. This was Sergio's team, not mine. But we were an organism nonetheless, and one that I had to keep alive at all costs. Whether or not I died in the process was beside the point.

I sensed that Cancer knew this too. Maybe not at the start of the mission, but he did now. He wasn't dressing me down in front of the team. His admonition that we may have to flee the Organization forever wasn't intended to intimidate me but to develop and guide me. He was sharing a candid reality so I'd be mentally and emotionally prepared to react if and when we found the one hope upon which we'd been staking our survival no longer there.

I checked my watch. "It's been thirty minutes. We're executing a two-man assault on Ribeiro's compound. Let's go."

* * *

As we marched north, the eastern tip of the clearing fell away behind us.

My mind wasn't murky or troubled by our loss; instead, I compartmentalized Sergio and Reilly. We didn't know what happened to them, so there was no point trying to guess. And the answer may not matter soon anyway: Cancer and I were following this path to the end of the line, all the way to a two-man raid. The very idea was suicide—but what else was new? Impossible odds had been the norm since the moment we slid down the fast rope and set foot in Argentina.

Cancer stopped walking suddenly. I slowed my pace, looking around to see why.

Suddenly a hard object snapped against my skull

above my right eye. It was as small as a bullet but hadn't killed me outright—surely a ricochet, though I should have been too far from the battle for that.

I took a few stumbling steps, whipping my rifle up to scan for threats when a pebble slammed into my sternum with maximum throwing force.

Then I saw Reilly on the high ground behind a tree, leering at me from his concealed position. He threw another pebble, this one snapping into my thigh before I could dodge it.

"Goddamnit!" I hissed. "That one almost hit me in the balls!"

He gave a mock shrug in return. "Just wanted to make sure I stopped you."

Sergio appeared from behind a tree next to him, raising a pebble to whip it at Cancer.

Cancer warned, "Don't make me shoot you, Serge."

Sergio lowered his hand and let the pebble drop to the ground.

We approached them and had a quick team huddle.

I asked, "What happened to eastern tip of the clearing?"

Reilly said, "You two were late. We were afraid you'd gotten captured and tortured to give up the location of your better half. So we offset a bit to make sure the Mongolian horde wasn't heading north to find us."

"What happened to the rant about the Outfit screening for people who can keep secrets under abuse?" I asked.

Sergio shrugged. "Trust but verify. Now, let's get moving. I want to be in position for the raid by sundown. If we can't penetrate the objective or Ribeiro's not there, that gives us a full period of darkness to start evading."

* * *

Darkness had already fallen when we located the cocaine lab.

I was watching Reilly through night vision when he halted and dropped to the ground. He lay prone, then crawled forward to get eyes on before waving the rest of us up to his position.

Conceptually, I knew we wouldn't find much—whether defunct or actively producing, jungle cocaine labs weren't synonymous with lavish accommodation.

But intuitively, I couldn't reconcile what I was seeing with any possibility that Ribeiro was ever there, much less currently waiting.

There was almost nothing to see. A few scattered structures, if you could call them that. Roofs of canvas or tarp stretched taut and angled downward to let rainwater flow off, held upright by the most rudimentary of wooden supports.

Only a few established positions had walls, and from a distance, even these appeared to be formed from crudely assembled wooden planks.

The guard force confounded me. There were sentries, yes—but only just so. I could make out seven of them from my vantage point, though a few more may have been tucked out of sight.

But professional soldiers they were not. The lack of a campfire was about their only concession to proper security. Other than that, they talked amongst themselves, ambling about the site with flashlights. A few sat in chairs facing the jungle, rifles resting casually across their laps.

I whispered to Cancer, "You need to relocate your sniper position?"

"What for?" he replied. "I could waste the whole camp right now. I'm staying right here."

"Let us get as close as we can before you start smoking dudes—we don't have the manpower to chase down any squirters."

"Ain't gonna be no squirters, boss. I promise you that."

"Give us a couple minutes to flank. We'll come in from the west."

I turned and crawled back into the jungle before leading Reilly and Sergio ten meters into the undergrowth for a quick brief.

"All right," I began. "We all know something's wrong down there. Any considerations before we assault?"

Sergio replied, "To me, the guard force looked expendable. Like someone posted them there to die."

Reilly noted, "Well that's convenient, because they're gonna."

Sergio continued, "I will say, their movement makes me confident they're not worried about stepping onto a booby trap."

I nodded. "So we can take them down fast, under night vision. Anything else?"

Reilly said, "Don't overthink it, boss. Let's go smash them."

And with that, we began our circling maneuver to flank toward the west side of the camp.

* * *

A pelting drizzle erupted as we prepared to break cover for our assault. Above the canopy, it was probably a downpour—but after sifting through layers of treetops, the rain was reduced to a saltshaker effect.

Reilly took point, with Sergio and me fanning out to

his side to establish fields of fire on the tiny encampment. We moved at a steady, stealthy pace, with no need to rush until we'd compromised ourselves to the guards.

My rifle felt cold in my hands. Something was wrong, though I couldn't put my finger on what. Within seconds adrenaline would take over as we assaulted forward, negating any ability for me to contemplate the situation. I looked forward to the reprieve, bitterly noting that this had become the story of my life— combat as sport, flinging myself into the unknown to achieve distraction.

Except this time, there were greater consequences than my own death. If Ribeiro wasn't in the camp, then we had no other options. The grand plan in progress would result in nothing more than my team's reduction to animals fleeing the slaughter of the hunt.

We were ten meters from the camp's perimeter when Reilly activated his infrared laser. The rope blazed neon green in our night vision, though it would be invisible to the naked eye. No response from the camp's occupants— our final confirmation that none of the guards had night vision.

Sergio and I activated our infrared lasers as well, our trio of beams scanning the lab until they located the nearest three guards. Then a fourth laser blazed in from our right: Cancer taking aim at the northernmost guard position, dedicating his most precise shot to the sentry most likely to escape.

No sooner had Cancer taken aim than the nearest sentry called out over the rain. A single shouted, indiscernible word preceded the beam of his flashlight slicing through the drizzle toward us, and Reilly halted abruptly to fire two rounds.

The man tumbled forward out of his chair, the flashlight arcing in slow-motion as its beam cartwheeled upward to the treetops.

I drilled two rounds into a man leaning against a structure. Sergio popped off three bullets to fell his target, and then we broke into a run.

Then the camp turned into a massacre, a pinball machine of death.

Cancer was smoking guards as quickly as I could locate them through my night vision. By the time I saw a human profile and raised my rifle, the man's head had whipped back and he dropped like a puppet with the strings cut. Cancer wanted his payback for Viggs, all right, and he was getting it one head shot at a time.

This wasn't combat, it was slaughter. Were it not for their rifles, we may as well have been shooting farmers. The previous days on the run and rolling gunfights had left our team primed for the worst, and this was almost too easy. Every round found its mark; our targets seemed impossible to miss.

A man broke north out of the camp, his flight into the jungle ended when I cracked a half-dozen rounds into his backside. Swinging my barrel back into the camp, I saw three men airborne—one trying to fling himself behind a structure as Reilly lit him up, two others falling lifeless to the ground after Cancer's and Sergio's fire found its mark.

Incredibly, one man came tumbling from under a tarp in a lunging run toward us. Whether valor or cowardice, I had no idea; I gut-shot him twice before he could crack off a bullet, then turned his falling body into a corpse with three more shots before he'd hit the ground.

We activated infrared floodlights at the camp's perimeter, bathing the structures before us in luminescent green. Then we swept through the camp, double-tapping each body we passed. All overhanging tarps and structure interiors were cleared on the move, our triple floodlights converging and spinning to indicate each man's coverage to the others.

I cleared under a tarp overhang, seeing only piles of supplies. Turning to fire twice into a corpse beside me, I sped up to keep in line with Sergio and Reilly. We found no additional men, no survivors, and no surprises— which, in this rare case, was an exceedingly bad thing.

"LOA!" Sergio called, signaling the limit of advance for our clearance.

With only three of us maneuvering, there would be no perimeter security; we all turned to begin searching the camp in earnest.

No sooner had I spun in place than I caught sight of Cancer racing downhill, out of the jungle. He slung his sniper rifle on his back, drawing a knife and descending on the nearest casualty like a Native American warrior taking scalps. But Cancer had no interest in war trophies; instead he was slashing throats and eviscerating men either already dead or mortally wounded.

I didn't try and stop him, and neither did Sergio. Whoever these guards were, they clearly had no intelligence value. Besides that, I felt I had no right to prevent any of my team from claiming whatever cathartic release they could.

We began searching. The vestiges of cocaine processing were all around—empty chemical jugs, open vats long since dried of their contents. Living supplies were likewise everywhere, but they were the bare essentials of poor men living in the jungle.

The rain stopped. There was still no sign of Ribeiro.

I called out, "White light everything!"

We flipped our night vision upward, turning on our rifles' blazing tactical lights. The camp illuminated in a spectrum of colors—blue tarps, rusty red barrels—and we began tearing everything apart. Every pack was opened, contents flung into the rain as we searched.

"I got something!" Reilly called.

He'd overturned a table and was stomping on the ground beneath it. We converged around him, finding there was indeed a panel beneath the earth. This was well-disguised, so carefully put into place that it could have easily escaped the attention of even the camp's occupants.

We kicked the dirt aside, exposing a flat panel of wood spreading five square feet. When we began to pry it upward, I saw sheets of plastic spread below—this was a good sign. Whatever the contents, they were valuable enough to weatherproof.

In our feverish rush to expose the cache, we clumsily knocked into one another.

Reilly shouted, "Gimme some room!"

We stepped back and Reilly ripped the wooden board upward. Sergio took it from him and tossed it to the side. I held my light steady over sheets of plastic as Reilly began slicing through them.

Suddenly Reilly fell onto his side, violently retching.

"Gas!" Sergio cried.

I grabbed Reilly and hauled him backward as we spread out, away from the hole. There was a booby trap after all, and a particularly insidious one—some nerve agent or chemical gas staged to wipe out the undeserving. It was fitting protection in the jungle, I thought bitterly— no one would be packing a gas mask unless they'd been specifically sent to recover the cache.

But Reilly cracked a fist into my forearm to break my grasp.

"Stop it, you"—he gagged and sputtered—"fucking idiot."

I dropped him in place. "What?"

"You—" he choked again. "It ain't—"

Then he began seizing into a coughing fit.

Sergio and Cancer were giving the hole a wide berth, remaining twenty feet distant as they watched me for guidance.

Taking a deep breath and holding the air in my lungs, I approached the hole.

My white light flooded across the plastic sheets gashed apart by Reilly's knife. Then I saw what lay below, and realized it was a good thing I was holding my breath.

It was a cache, all right. The main contents were shrink-wrapped bricks of US dollars, stacks of them piled on top of one another. Without a doubt, I was looking at millions. Most of the stacks were intact, though a few had been sliced open to leave scattered bundles of cash in disarray. Many bundles were clearly missing—someone had taken all they could carry and vanished into the jungle.

But the resulting extra space was not empty; it had been filled with a deposit of a different sort.

Even with my breath held, a putrid, roast-pork smell tingled within my nostrils. The source wasn't gas from a booby trap, as Sergio initially suspected.

It was rotting human flesh.

A body lay amid the cash, decomposed almost beyond recognition. Almost, I realized, but not entirely—the thick-lens glasses that canted across the discolored, formerly rotund face were immediately recognizable.

This was Ribeiro.

His cause of death was clear enough—his throat slit exactly as Viggs's had been.

I took a few steps back to gasp a breath as Cancer approached.

"Now we know why they set a trap with Viggs," he said. "They didn't have the manpower to overrun us. Just like we thought."

Sergio edged forward to look into the hole.

Cancer's face was illuminated from the glow of our tac lights as he spoke again. "Agustin wasn't trying to find and kill us. He was trying to buy time with limited forces so he could make his escape." He shrugged. "Now he's gone."

I nodded distantly, knowing Cancer was right. That was why the camp was so lightly guarded. Agustin had killed Ribeiro, taking both his commanding role and most of the forces. Had this coup been a long time coming, or had Agustin made a snap judgment when he felt the Handler's forces drawing too near?

We killed our white lights and stumbled away from the hole, trying to escape the smell.

Reilly was the first to speak. "We can't go back."

"What do you mean?" I said. "We got Ribeiro."

Cancer corrected, "Agustin got Ribeiro. They ain't going to let us return alive, one way or the other."

"They're right," Sergio said. "We can't go back like this, Suicide. Not after we got Outfit guys killed back there."

Reilly said, "The more I see of how the Organization works, the more I'm certain that they don't care if we killed Hitler, much less Ribeiro. We disobeyed orders, period. They're going to kill us and turn it into a three-ring circus to send a message about what happens to shooters who go rogue."

Cancer added, "The Handler assembled this team for a reason; if we return to the US, he'll kill us for that same reason. We need to disappear down here."

"I don't need to disappear," I said boldly, my voice more forceful than I intended.

Sergio looked to me sadly. "You more than anyone, brother."

"I'm tired of letting the Handler win." But for the first time, I saw a way to defeat him. Not to kill him, regrettably, but to outmaneuver him on his own playing field.

And to do so required Parvaneh.

Sergio cautioned, "Don't be stubborn about this, Suicide. We should leave now, start heading—"

"Stop it!" I nearly shouted. Quieting my voice, I went on, "I don't want to hear any more."

Cancer stepped closer to me. "Who do you think you are?"

I drew a long breath. "I'm telling you to stop talking because I don't want to know where you'll go. Because I'm headed back home."

Sergio clutched his rifle. "You're dead if you do."

"Maybe. Or maybe"—I thought of Parvaneh—"I'll be able to secure your safe return."

Reilly swung his head to me. "Because of his daughter?"

"Because I'm a good bullshitter."

Sergio spoke quickly. "Don't kill yourself for us. The cash in that hole changes everything. We can live for a long time off that money. We'll find a place to live, find some *mamacitas*...it won't be so bad."

I shook my head. "For years, teams have served the Handler and then been exiled to Latin America for their troubles. That's not going to happen to you guys, I promise you. And I'll put my head on the chopping block to ensure it. I'll turn myself over, give a version of our story that the Handler has no choice but to accept in public.

You guys keep the satellite phone that we took from those spotters. Once the coast is clear, I'll call you."

Sergio pointed out, "You can't write down the number."

"I memorized a phone number for the Handler and didn't forget it in eight months until I needed it most. And I'm not"—I nodded to the group—"forgetting it in the month or so it'll take me to make sure you guys will be safe upon return."

"What if they torture you?"

"The Outfit screens for people who can withstand questioning." I slapped Cancer on the shoulder. "If I can take a few cigarette burns without talking, I can take this number to the grave. Believe me, I won't call until I'm certain it's safe for your return. Think you can survive until then?"

"We've put up with you for the past three days," Cancer said. "Finding a spot to lie low for a while will be a breeze."

They took turns holding their breath to haul cash out of the hole, filling their packs with as much as they could carry. I stood immobile, holding the satellite phone and reading the number printed on the back of it over and over. Once I'd committed it to memory, I closed my eyes and recited it in my mind.

Sergio said, "We're out of here, boss."

I opened my eyes to see the three men standing before me. Cancer held his hand out, and I handed him the satellite phone.

He asked, "Sure you got this memorized?"

"I got it. You guys want to split up my gear?"

Sergio shook his head. "It will be suspicious if you're missing too much equipment. The best thing you can give us, Suicide, is an explanation to the Outfit that we're probably dead."

"I'll come up with something," I promised. "Just wait for my call."

Reilly said, "Until next time, boss."

He held up his fist and I knocked my knuckles against it, repeating the process for Cancer and Sergio.

Without another word, they turned and moved out into the jungle.

And after a long mission spent on the run with my team, I was finally alone. I wondered when I'd see them again, or even if I would—what if they never answered my call? But, I assured myself, these guys had made it through a lot and would make it through a lot more, particularly with the cash they'd just liberated from Ribeiro's grave. Wherever they were headed, and however they intended to survive in the interim, I'd get them out of here alive. The Suicide Cartel would be reconstituted on American soil, would return home alive after Viggs's sacrifice.

It was spooky watching them fade into the mist and then being left alone in the night amid the acidic stench of a decomposing corpse and the dead guards all around me. Ghosts weren't real, until they were—Ribeiro was dead, but Agustin was still out there. He'd slayed his own king and fled...where was he now?

I set up my satellite antenna, orienting it to an open patch in the treetops. Then I transmitted.

"Halo One, this is Tomcat Actual."

"Tomcat Actual, this is Halo One, send your traffic."

"Tomcat element confirms jackpot, Objective Ribeiro."

A long pause this time. Who would have guessed?

"Say again, Tomcat."

"I say again: Tomcat confirms jackpot, Objective Ribeiro."

A different voice this time. Some supervisor had snatched the mic away from a radio operator.

"Killed or captured?"

"Killed. Tomcat requests immediate recovery and exfil. Target has been cleared, advise recovery element do not shoot, I say again DO NOT SHOOT. How copy?"

"Good copy. Send your grid."

I transmitted the grid, then added, "Tomcat will be unarmed. Will surrender to any Outfit recovery forces. Do not shoot, copy?"

"Copy. Are all members of Tomcat element accounted for?"

I swallowed. "Roger that. Send the pickup."

I turned and stared into the jungle, a murky green haze under my night vision. My thoughts darted to the wire diagram of Ribeiro's organization, how I'd been shocked to see how high a position Agustin occupied, countered by his presence on the kill team that pursued Parvaneh into the Rio slum.

Another thought occurred to me, one that I couldn't substantiate any more than Cancer's suspicion that Agustin had orchestrated Viggs's macabre death to lure us in because he didn't have the manpower to pursue us.

But the thought was this: Agustin had led the kill team into the favela not just because he enjoyed it, though that was certainly a factor, but also because he wanted to

personally ensure that Parvaneh was killed by any means necessary. He did so not for pleasure, but rather because he had made a promise to some hidden sponsor. And when he failed to kill her at the initial ambush in Rio, he'd tried to clean his mess any way he could.

Ribeiro had appeared genuine at his meeting with Parvaneh precisely because he *was* genuine—a business-man, whereas Agustin was overcome with the ruthless ambition that caused him to toy with me when he thought I'd be killed within the hour.

Do you see our Redeemer?

Troubled by the thought, I began stripping myself naked over the waist to await the Outfit's arrival. They'd see I was unarmed, but the last thing I needed was to get shot for suspicion of wearing a suicide vest. I began to shiver as the rain hit my exposed skin.

Then I closed my eyes, reciting the number to the satellite phone over and over in my mind.

10

September 9, 2009
The Mist Palace
British Columbia, Canada

And here I was, right back in the Handler's de facto courtroom.

I was overcome with an eerie sense of déjà vu—just as I'd returned from battle in Myanmar to be brought here, so too did my journey from the Triple Frontier lead to this dead end, where those who did were judged by those who didn't. Just as on my first visit here, the three chief vicars were seated—Watts, Omari, and Yosef. The Handler was once more perched atop the high seat with Parvaneh at his right side, both backed by their personal bodyguards. Only a few guards were present, exceptionally low security that was no doubt intended to minimize witnesses to the proceedings.

This time, however, there were a few key differences.

A young, freckled woman now occupied the speaker podium once belonging to the late Ishway. Large framed glasses hovered over her childlike features, the image of youth enhanced by hair cut in a short bob. She looked young enough to be a graduate student, and I took her for an intellectual prodigy of some kind.

Most significantly, Parvaneh didn't avoid my eyes this time around. But her face registered shock when she first saw me. I couldn't understand why, until I recalled the sight that had greeted me in my shaving mirror. I'd lost ten pounds in the jungle, my eyes sunken even though I'd slept nearly the entire plane ride back to North America.

But after her initial shock, Parvaneh met my gaze calmly and frequently. She exuded a confidence that I couldn't share, seeming certain we could pull off the delicate balancing act that was about to transpire. But I, having a singularly different history with her father, could sense only an imminent fall to destruction.

Was there such a thing as winning in this game? My team, the Suicide Cartel, had been sent to death. We'd barely succeeded in staying alive, much less reaching Ribeiro; and even then, I was the sole representative facing the Handler's wrath for not dying as intended.

I had to kill him. I *had* to. I knew not how or when, but this had to be done. Even if it was the last thing I ever did —maybe especially so. Whether I won or lost in the current proceedings, the Handler would have prevailed by virtue of remaining alive.

I could read his eyes like a picture book: he knew that I'd figured out his entire ploy, could tell from the delicate manner I'd attempted repatriation. If my team had followed orders in South America, we'd have been killed by the enemy; if we didn't follow orders, we'd be killed by the Organization. Either way, the Handler won. I could see from his face that he knew I wanted to kill him, now more than ever.

And he didn't care, because he knew I couldn't.

I would prove him wrong.

It now went beyond simple revenge; I knew the evil he represented, the evil he perpetuated across the globe.

But this logic held a significant counterpoint.

I'd been on the path of revenge for over a year, and couldn't discount the enormity of what I'd done in that time. When Ian approached me with a way to kill the Handler, I was a twenty-five-year-old kid with exactly three mercenary operations under my belt. Since then I'd infiltrated the Outfit, deployed to Somalia and Brazil and Myanmar, and furthered a plot against the Handler before singlehandedly ending it to prevent the greater tragedy of massacred civilians. Even the mission from which I'd just emerged represented the polar opposite of where I'd begun: commander of an Outfit team sent on a cross-border suicide mission in Argentina, yet emerging with all but one of my men alive.

All but one.

The thought stung me, and I suppressed a vivid recollection of Viggs as I last saw him, as I would be destined to remember him no matter how hard I tried to avoid it. The Handler deserved to die for Viggs alone, much less his litany of sins against those sent into battle to wage war on his behalf.

But deserving to die didn't mean I was able to kill him, and I had over a year of attempts to prove it. That distinction was perhaps the greatest single lesson I'd learned. Getting as close to the Handler as I had was an achievement, perhaps unprecedented—ultimately futile, but an achievement nonetheless. I'd provoked his entire security apparatus on multiple occasions while continuing to process oxygen into carbon dioxide, and that put me in a league of my own from the army of failed assassins who'd since found early graves.

Now I was face-to-face with him once more, this time as a rogue agent with a trump card. The Handler couldn't probe too far into my motivations without revealing to his daughter that he'd sent me to die, and I had to tap dance around the truth to avoid being dismissed as a treasonous liar.

It would be a delicate balancing act between us, and that act was about to begin.

The young woman with the bob cut addressed me. "Mr. Rivers, my name is Fiona." Her eyes behind the glasses were wide and sparkling with intelligence. "I will be asking you a series of questions regarding the mission from which you've just returned."

I felt a spike of alertness—a distinct nervousness about getting outsmarted and trapped in interrogation by the Handler's newest whiz kid. But I harbored a far deeper understanding of the situation than she.

"I will speak the truth," I said. My first lie.

"Let's begin with the infiltration. You directed the pilots to divert to your emergency rope point. Why?"

"I had a bad feeling about the primary."

"A bad...feeling?" I sensed an air of apprehension in her voice now, and took this to be her first such performance in the Handler's court.

"Yes."

"Based on what?"

"I don't know. That's why I said 'feeling' and not 'fact.'"

"So you took it upon yourself to alter the mission profile?"

"I was ground force commander. That's my right." She was watching me closely, maybe uncertain if I was finished or maybe unsatisfied with my answer. So I concluded, "You want to do my job, I'll swap you

202

paychecks and stand behind that podium to do yours. Let me know how you fare in the Triple Frontier."

"David," Watts barked, his facial scars straining with anger, "that's enough. You're still representing the Outfit."

I shot him a wry glance. Representing the Outfit, indeed. The Outfit, a band of war vets exploited for the financial ends of people who didn't trouble themselves with the outcome. Watts chief among them, whether he lectured me on respecting this kangaroo court or not. With a flash of contempt, I realized that Watts hadn't served a single day in the Outfit. He couldn't have, or he'd be unable to subject those men to what they encountered in the Handler's service. Watts hadn't come up through the Outfit ranks like Sergio had. Instead, he'd been plucked from the upper echelons of one military branch or another and then given control here.

I said nothing in response to Watts, returning my eyes to Fiona instead. She hadn't budged, and continued speaking with remarkable tenacity.

"After sending your situation report of enemy contact, your element then operated over forty-eight hours without establishing communications to your head-quarters."

I nodded. "Following that report, we were under almost continuous enemy contact. We spent the next two days in rolling gunfights with pursuing forces. On the rare occasions that we weren't at risk of imminent death, our communications were sporadic by virtue of the jungle canopy. It was difficult to dial in the satellite."

"Describe the enemy forces you encountered."

"There were two main elements, as far as we could tell. First was the local cartel militia, outfitted in local garb, with tracking dogs and access to a spotter network. Latin American appearance. Then there was a significant element of Arabs that we presumed to be Hezbollah. They wore tiger-stripe camouflage, and were well-trained and equipped with night vision."

Then I swallowed, blinking quickly as I laced truth with fiction. "We couldn't shake them. Every time we broke contact and conducted evasive maneuvers, we'd try to continue mission, but one element or the other would find us. Eventually we'd been forced so far from our reconnaissance objective that I had no choice but to abort the mission. After that, we were trying to stay alive long enough to make radio communications."

"When did you sustain casualties?"

"Viggs was wounded early on, and..." I trailed off, riveted by the wood grain on the table before me.

"Go on, Mr. Rivers," Fiona directed.

I took a breath. "We carried him in a litter. He'd taken a bayonet to the gut saving my life."

"And then?"

I raised my eyes to Fiona. My gaze must have spoken that I could've strangled her for probing for further information, but I managed to keep my voice reasonably level as I continued.

"We transported Viggs in a litter, had to hide him for an uphill movement to gather intelligence on our route. When we returned...he'd been killed. Rigged hanging from a tree by Ribeiro's operations officer, Agustin."

"How can you be certain it was Agustin?"

"He left me a message."

"That message was?"

I sighed. "'Do you see our Redeemer.' Written on Viggs's body in blood. It was from a conversation he and I had in Rio, before he tried to kill Parvaneh."

Fiona looked troubled by this. "How could Agustin have known you were on the recon team?"

I didn't look at the Handler, though not doing so represented the outer boundaries of my willpower.

Instead I responded, "My name, and my name only, was found on a note from a dead Hezbollah fighter. How they knew me, I have no idea. But I suspect Agustin had sources that knew whatever Hezbollah did, and he chose to send a reminder of Rio."

"Then what?"

"The four of us made a river crossing, trying to lose our pursuers. We encountered another Hezbollah element and tried to evade the way we'd come, but the cartel was closing in. Sergio had a leg injury and was having trouble moving. We could no longer outrun our pursuers. I managed to send out a comms shot to request emergency rescue. Headquarters confirmed our location, so we set up a defense and waited."

"What happened then?"

"Then the world closed in around us."

"And what does that mean, exactly?"

I looked at her again. Her gaze was cold. Mine wasn't.

"It means we got hit from all sides."

"Attacked?"

"It was total chaos. There was no way we could defend ourselves. We tried to fight our way north along a ravine. Then there was an explosion. Black smoke. We...we lost sight of Sergio and Reilly."

"'We' being who, Mr. Rivers?"

"Cancer and me."

She looked confused as she referenced her notes. "You mean Alan?"

I smirked without meaning to. "Alan to you. Cancer to me. But yes—Cancer and I continued along the ravine, somehow escaping the gunfire behind us, and kept running north. We were still evading when we encountered the camp."

"If the two of you were running for your lives, why not bypass the camp?"

"We agreed something wasn't right."

"How, exactly?"

"Every enemy on the face of the earth was involved in fighting just south of there, practically within earshot." I swallowed. "But here, we could see sentries defending a few scattered shacks. Cancer and I agreed the enemy disposition indicated the presence of a significant high-value target, someone who didn't have the remaining network to continue running. This was consistent with reports of the executive staff abandoned when Ribeiro supposedly fled the continent."

"But you didn't report this. Notably, you did not call in—"

"Of course not. We'd just escaped the shootout of a lifetime and didn't know how long we had before we were overrun. We decided to inflict the maximum damage to the Organization's enemies that we could, and staged a hasty raid. Cancer burned down the guards with his sniper rifle while I maneuvered."

"And then?"

"We initiated contact with a crossfire that dropped every member of the ground force. Cancer was supposed to join me then, so we could clear the camp together. But he didn't come and I couldn't raise him on radio, so I proceeded alone."

"You cleared the encampment alone?"

"That's correct," I answered simply.

Fiona looked flustered by my response, her freckled cheeks coloring in anticipation. She had to press me further, but dreaded the possibility of a smartass response. This emotion played upon her features, making her appear more woman than girl. Given a few years to mature and get some self-confidence, I thought, she'd be quite pretty.

"Well, why did you act alone?"

"Sweetheart, if you're going to ask 'why' so often, you've got a long road ahead in trying to understand the Outfit."

A low, rolling chuckle from Omari. Watts looked furious.

Fiona held her ground with considerable poise, seamlessly continuing, "And what then?"

"None of the dead enemies were recognizable high-value targets. The next logical conclusion was that they were in place to defend a cache of some kind, so I began searching."

"And your search uncovered the underground space."

"Correct. It was well concealed; I was lucky to find it. Piles of cash that someone had raided in a hurry. And Ribeiro's body, likely a few days into decomposition. But that wasn't what troubled me."

"And what troubled you, Mr. Rivers?"

"Two things. First: I couldn't reach Cancer. He still wouldn't answer the radio, and when I flanked back toward his sniper position, I couldn't find him. I located the expended brass from the shots he'd fired, but he was gone. Captured, for all I know."

"And the second thing that bothered you?"

"Agustin was gone. And while I can't state this for certain, I think he was responsible for the betrayal of Parvaneh's delegation in Rio. Not Ribeiro. It is my personal belief that Agustin didn't act alone, but rather with the influence of some hidden sponsor with whom he'd forged an alliance."

"Whom do you suspect this sponsor to be, Mr. Rivers?"

"I haven't the least idea. But that's what my gut tells me. Agustin killed Ribeiro for a reason, not because he wasn't prepared to deal with the consequences."

Omari intervened.

"In your transmission, you were asked if all members of your team were accounted for. You responded in the affirmative. How do you explain this...discrepancy?"

The three vicars were watching me closely; I could tell this was a point of contention they'd debated long before my return. A valid point, I noted, because they were trying to determine whether anyone from my team was still alive.

"There was a lot of overhead cover, and the transmission was coming in broken. I must have misheard."

Yosef looked unconvinced; he was smart enough to know better. Watts and Omari were expressionless, though I knew they could prove nothing.

I dared not look at the Handler for fear of appearing as if I sought his approval for my version of events.

But the Handler addressed me a moment later, commanding my stare.

"We have recorded enemy transmissions reporting the capture of Viggs. You are correct, David. It was Agustin who ordered Viggs executed, his body violated." He looked to Fiona, and my heart began slamming. "Play the recording—"

"I don't need to hear it," I said, trying to control the dreadful guilt in my voice. I should have leapt at the chance to learn more. Instead, I felt every raging undertow of suppressed PTSD surging to the surface with the memory of seeing Viggs dead. Hearing a recording of Agustin's voice would have caused me a full meltdown. "I know it was Agustin."

The Handler seemed to sense my emotion, and mercifully changed the topic. But mercy wasn't in his wheelhouse, which intrigued me further as he went on, "And we know from your testimony after the Rio de Janeiro delegation that Agustin personally led a kill team into the favela to assassinate Parvaneh."

"I remember."

"I take it that Agustin's death is a goal you would stop at nothing to achieve."

"That is a fair estimate." And unlike the Handler himself, I thought, with Agustin I had a shot of making it work.

"I have conferred with the Chief Vicar of Defense and prepared an assignment commensurate with your Outfit career progression as well as your personal motivations."

I bit. "I look forward to hearing the opportunity, sir."

"We now offer you command of a special task force with one mission: to locate, then capture or kill, Agustin Villalba. Together with the Outfit commander, you will handpick your men. Including Ian, if you so choose." The possibilities of a handpicked team startled me—I could recover the Suicide Cartel from their exile, even bring Ian out of his forced retirement.

What a formidable force we would be.

The Handler continued, "Your funding and resources to accomplish this task will be virtually limitless. And you will have top advisors to assist you in crafting a campaign plan, with tactical command of all subsidiary operations."

"What about missions?" I asked impulsively.

"You have full authority to operate on any or all missions of your choosing. With support platforms for infiltration by air, land, or water as you deem fit."

I looked to Watts, whose unflinching glare spoke four words to me: *you don't deserve this.* Of course he thought that—he hadn't wanted me in charge of a single Outfit team, much less a task force. He'd probably had a field day with the assignment to hunt us down in Argentina, and now he was watching me get promoted.

By contrast, the Handler looked as placid and assured as ever. Of course he would. Every indication from our interactions and my psychological profile, much less the access of his surveillance devices, had indicated that I would choose continued Outfit service. This calculus had allowed the Handler to take the strategic risk of giving me a fair offer before his court, thus recovering his reputation before I besmirched it publicly with irrefutable evidence of the suicide mission. Because the true court he cared about was his daughter's opinion—and that was the one thing I could affect.

And he couldn't have known that Parvaneh and I had spoken in private, because he was unaware she had a secret path to visit me.

"All that remains," the Handler continued, "is for you to accept. You may then begin the hunt for Agustin as soon as you wish."

I drew a breath and closed my eyes, sealing the world to blackness. I now had to commit to my final decision, and do so in opposition to every instinct I possessed. But those instincts had led me where I was today with precious little to show for it.

The pursuit of combat, much less revenge, would destroy me. It was a miracle one or both hadn't done so already. And yet I'd managed to be a savior on two occasions: to Ian, and to the Suicide Cartel.

Now I was ruined myself, a self-made slave to adrenaline and combat as much as any external oppressor.

Now I needed Parvaneh to save me.

Opening my eyes, I looked into the Handler's amber

irises. "I am deeply grateful for your gracious consideration, and the trust you show in me." He nodded as I continued, "But I don't want to remain in the Outfit. I choose to join Parvaneh's delegation instead." Looking to her, I gave a brief nod and vowed, "I'm done fighting."

"After your history with the father of her child, I don't think that—"

"I accept," Parvaneh declared.

You could have heard a pin drop in the next room following her words, but she'd spoken them matter-of-factly, without room for debate. Now she sat regally as ever, as if the matter was settled.

"Parvaneh," the Handler said. "You cannot be serious."

"The delegation is mine to run as I see fit. David has just retired from the Outfit. That makes him available for other purposes, does it not?"

Watts cleared his throat, seemingly to save the Handler the embarrassment of a vocal confrontation with his daughter. Then Watts said, "David is not a diplomat, nor does he have the skills to serve as an aide. He is a fighter, ma'am. Nothing more."

Parvaneh nodded to Watts, as if this deduction were the most brilliant notion yet spoken in the court. "Well said, Vicar Watts. And who better to advise those that send our warriors into combat than someone who has seen the battlefield himself?"

Watts's face reddened as he forced his mouth shut.

Now it was Omari's turn to intervene. "These are trying times for our Organization. The danger has never been greater, and I submit that this is not the time to take chances with our diplomatic efforts."

Again, Parvaneh nodded in gracious concession. "We are in agreement about the danger. But David has saved my life once." She looked to me, then back at Omari. "He can do it again."

The Handler was silent for a moment, expressionless —and this was my first indication that we'd won. Beneath that placid exterior loomed a deep embarrassment and fury that he wouldn't risk betraying in a public setting. Parvaneh and I had just outmaneuvered him before his court and in a manner inconceivable to any element of his extensive security network.

Now, he couldn't back out.

Fiona appeared to be taking this all in, trying to make sense of what had just happened. She'd stood at the podium nervous about her own performance, and now she was seeing her new masters restless and unsettled with the sudden turn of events. Did she realize these men were evil? Was she beginning to sense it now, or was she too blinded by greed?

The Handler's eyes widened momentarily, and he began rubbing his cheekbone with index and middle fingers joined. I could tell he wanted to end this charade and escape the courtroom before his last vestige of control slipped away.

"Very well." The words seemed to stick in his throat.

Parvaneh looked to me. "David, get some rest. My delegation departs at daybreak. We will conduct your initial counseling aboard the plane."

"Yes, ma'am," I replied.

And with that, court was adjourned.

* * *

It was well past sundown when Parvaneh finally entered my room.

She did so in the same manner that she had before my

departure for Argentina—entering a key code, slipping inside, and quietly shutting the door behind her. Certain that she hadn't been seen, absolutely confident in her ability to come and go without detection despite the myriad security measures in place throughout the Mist Palace.

She said nothing; she didn't need to. Our eyes spoke in the pregnant pause before we undressed each other— we'd planned an unprecedented deception, I'd returned from South America against all odds, and now the Handler was publicly cornered into allowing my assignment to her delegation.

In doing so, I'd been freed from an endless struggle of war and revenge.

Or had I?

I still wanted the Handler dead, now perhaps more than ever. I likewise craved the opportunity to slay Agustin. In some ways the two were one and the same: both carved from a blend of power and ruthlessness, creating a vision of evil perfected. Both totally committed to their cause, neither acknowledging any sanctity of human life in the balance. There was simply nothing they wouldn't sacrifice to pursue their ends, nothing sacred to them save the power they sought to claim.

It was no matter now, I lied to myself; now Parvaneh stood naked before me, and we made love for the second time. In a way ours was a union of perfect synthesis between opposites—me representing the worst of a better outside world, and her representing the best of a syndicate that existed in the shadows yet secretly governed so much.

Both of us had lost previous loves to the other's cause. We had every right to hate each other for past slights, and yet we instead found union along every possible fissure line—her authority and my servitude to the same Organization, my dedication to war and hers to diplomacy, her single-minded intention to reform the criminal underworld and my skepticism that she could do so. In a way our union with one another—whether sexual, romantic, or in ideology—represented the best of the human condition, the essence of forgiveness and future over attempting to punish the sins of the past.

These thoughts were wiped from my mind as we made love, a metaphorical cleansing of the horrors I'd witnessed in South America and elsewhere. Parvaneh was giving to me far more than she took; her body was purifying, a healing presence that permeated the core of my being.

After we finished she sat up on one elbow, her emerald eyes fixed upon mine.

"I know you withheld things from the court. And I am quite certain my father did as well. What really happened in Argentina, David?"

God, how I wanted to tell her. But I didn't need the catharsis of retelling events better forgotten; instead, I needed her help in securing the return of the Suicide Cartel. Sergio, Reilly, and Cancer were still out there while I lounged in the luxury of a bed, warm and dry with a woman at my side.

But the Handler was too volatile right now—after being trounced in court, I didn't know what he would plan next. No, instead I would depart with Parvaneh's delegation the next morning and, far from the Mist Palace, privately confide in her. She'd know how to negotiate the tightrope spanning the immense void between human dignity and her father's throne, and bring my team home at last.

"Parvaneh, I give you my word that I'll tell you the

entire story." Then I shook my head, squeezing her hand. "But not tonight. Okay?"

"As you wish, David. I'm just glad you're back."

"Me too."

"I've lost love once." She rubbed the back of her neck. "I couldn't bear to do so again."

"You won't have to," I assured her. "I'm a member of a peaceful delegation, remember? Totally domesticated."

"Think you can manage to stay sane in such a capacity?"

"I know I can." I gave her a reassuring smile and then felt my gaze drop with the sudden return of the memory I'd never fully forget.

Viggs's body, a dangling inverted crucifix twisting at the end of a rope. *Do you see our Redeemer?* Agustin wouldn't get a free pass, I told myself—after his many crimes, he'd be hunted down and killed by someone in the Handler's organization.

But it wouldn't be me.

The simple truth churned at the pit of my stomach, perhaps trounced by one worse: the Handler was going to live. Seemingly forever. And he would do so despite wiping out Boss's team, despite placing the Suicide Cartel into an impossibly fatal situation while sitting safe within his castle walls. He'd continue to live not because he deserved it, but because he was too well-protected for me to do anything else.

She asked, "What's wrong?"

"Nothing at all. I'm just tired, that's it. Glad to be back."

"There could be many possible answers to my question about what is wrong, but 'nothing at all' is not one of them."

"What's that supposed to mean?"

"You've just returned from war. And retired as a

warrior. Either one is an immensely difficult adjustment; both at once, even more so."

"I'm fine, I promise."

She ran her fingers through my hair, rubbing them across my head and letting them settle at the base of my neck. "Transitioning into diplomacy—into anything—after what you've been through is going to take time. But we'll figure it out together, and I will be there for you every step of the way. No matter how hard it gets."

I noticed my fingers beginning to tremble, and flexed my hand open and closed. "Nothing has been asked of me that hasn't been asked of anyone else in the Outfit, Parvaneh."

"I know. And every man will have to find his own path to salvation."

"Or not."

"Or not. But I'm here for you, and I always will be. You understand?"

I felt the sting of tears for no reason at all, then blinked them away before they became visible to her.

She leaned toward me and we kissed a final time before she rose from the bed. I propped my head up and watched her get dressed. Noticing my gaze, she continued to put on her garments with an air of grace.

I asked her, "You're sure you can come and go from here unseen?"

"Why do you ask?"

"Because if not, your father may dispose of me before morning."

"Oh ye of little faith. If I didn't have a way to come and go unseen, I wouldn't have come here in the first place."

"Good. So when do I get to meet your daughter, Langley?"

She stopped buttoning her blouse abruptly, then

smiled to herself. "Let's see how you do on your first delegation. Before I introduce you to my daughter, I have to be certain I won't fire you."

"Fair enough." I smiled.

Parvaneh finished buttoning her blouse and cast me a last look. Her eyes conveyed relief that I'd returned safely to her, an expression that she made no attempt to hide.

"Goodnight, David."

"Goodnight, Parvaneh."

I watched her from bed as she approached the door, entering a code into the keypad to open the deadbolt. Then she pushed the door open and stepped outside, quickly cutting left in the night as it slowly swung shut behind her.

Still naked, I burst out of bed and ran to the heavy metal door. Crouching beside it, I braced my hands to stop it from closing. It halted with a fraction of an inch of space remaining. Reaching behind the cabinet beside the door, I recovered a thin wedge of wood that I'd hidden there. Then, after slipping it in the gap between the door and its frame, I eased my fingers out to ensure the lock wouldn't re-engage.

I leapt to my feet, clumsily fighting my way into a pair of pants before reaching into the cabinet drawer to recover my night vision device.

Not bothering to put boots on for fear of losing her, I stormed to the door and paused for a moment to listen. Hearing nothing, I eased it open and peered left in the direction Parvaneh had departed.

I caught a glimpse of her sliding into a dark grove of trees. Only then did I commit to slipping outside. Letting the door ease shut against the wooden wedge, I hurried after her.

I was completely exposed now, shirtless and barefoot,

to whatever security measures awaited outside. My mind screamed that I was placing myself in a kill-on-sight position to any guard that happened to see me, a lunatic racing half naked through the Mist Palace compound.

But I trusted Parvaneh's words to me—that she had a way, that she was the only one who'd seen this fort through the eyes of a child. Did she mean herself or Langley?

It didn't matter now, I thought as I traced her path to the grove of trees. I turned on my night vision device, raising it to my eye to scan. I saw her then, a murky green silhouette walking down a pathway.

I followed as distantly as I could while keeping her in sight. My feet were tender and blistered from the Triple Frontier mission, each bare footfall an exercise in enduring pain as silently as possible. One errant noise could betray me, and I'd have no excuse—I would have betrayed Parvaneh's trust forever, would have destroyed the one good thing I had going for me, the only thing I'd achieved in the entire journey of vengeance I'd just renounced.

And yet, a deep instinctive urge propelled me forward. A secret pathway existed within the walls of the Handler's fortress, and against all logic I *needed* to know what it was.

But when I arrived at the grove of trees, I could no longer see her. I scanned a full 360, looking for any movement but seeing none. No buildings near enough for her to have disappeared into, unless she'd broken into a run without me noticing. I cast my vision downward, scanning the green field of view for some trapdoor or manhole cover in the foliage. But there wasn't one; just plants and rocks, the same as everywhere else. Then I looked up, searching the trees for a ladder or rope bridge. Nothing.

Where the fuck had she gone?

The eyes of a child.

I fell to my knees in despair, planting my hands against the earth to look low through the brush. That's when I saw it: one of the low flat stones that appeared to be flush with the ground had a hollowed-out slick of dirt carved out beneath it. What choice did I have? I crawled into it, the bottom of the stone scraping my back as I clumsily pulled myself forward through a short, rocky cavern.

The hollow ended at a wall, flat enough to be man-made though I knew it couldn't possibly be so. Before I had time to examine further, I saw a hole in the ground where the pathway ended. Fearful that I'd lose her, I slithered across cold mud toward it and lowered myself down into places unknown.

My bare feet came to rest on solid earth. What I saw reminded me of meeting Kun in Myanmar, where he'd mysteriously appeared in the cavern of a Buddhist shrine. I'd known then, had said so to Kun: *A person of your stature wouldn't be meeting at a dead end. You've got the closest thing to becoming invisible: a hidden tunnel.*

Why hadn't I suspected it for Parvaneh?

The space in which I crouched was not a natural cavern, but rather a square-shaped tunnel extending in both directions. Looking to my right, I saw the receding glow of a white light—Parvaneh had come prepared.

I scuttled after her, trying to quiet my footfalls as I observed the impossible. Wooden beams braced the tunnel walls—crude and having long ago fallen into disrepair, but wooden beams all the same. Yet Parvaneh couldn't have constructed this herself, nor could anyone else without the Handler's knowledge. Then I remembered what Sage had told me about the Mist Palace.

Somewhere in the Cascades of British Columbia... an

old settlement in ruins... and then I recalled the statement that explained it all.

Built at the site of an abandoned mining community from the Cariboo Gold Rush. Mid-1800s.

I was traveling through an ancient mining tunnel, one whose access points were so overgrown that only an inquisitive child would have the perspective to discover them.

Suddenly the light ahead stopped moving, spinning backward to cast a blinding glare down the tunnel toward me. I threw my back against the rough surface of the wall, holding my breath and not daring to risk the light glinting off the lenses of my night vision device.

The white light continued to stare in my direction, then turned and continued moving. I waited a moment, until the light extinguished altogether.

Creeping forward, I reached the location where the light had vanished.

Now I understood the end of the tunnel nearest my room, but where could Parvaneh have entered unseen? She was always watched, so was the Handler—in all places except one, I recalled.

Sage's voice again: *There is only one place the Handler or Parvaneh ventures alone, free from the immediate presence of guards.*

Sure enough, there was an opening in the tunnel ceiling representing little more than a space between rock fall but big enough for an adult to clamber through. Upward I went, sliding along its length to places unknown. Rock surfaces abraded the skin on my chest, and I could feel the sting of cold mud entering fresh cuts as I continued maneuvering toward the surface.

The hole in the earth where the tunnel emerged was overhung by another flat rock like the one concealing the entrance, and I crawled through the heavy undergrowth beyond it. Stopping to listen for movement, I indeed heard footsteps leading away. Frantic that I'd lose sight of Parvaneh, I rose to a knee, then found the vegetation thick enough that I could stand in relative concealment.

From Sage I'd demanded to know where the Handler and Parvaneh went alone. And Sage had replied coyly: *You're the self-proclaimed strategist, David. You tell me.*

I caught sight of Parvaneh's figure for a final time. Her light was off as she followed a paved trail, sauntering along as if on a daylight park stroll. I made a move to pursue, then caught sight of something beside me that made me stop altogether. I would follow her no farther—I knew exactly where I was, and recognized that she was about to pass back through the threshold of security.

The garden, I'd replied to Sage. *The fortress within a fortress that I saw after coming back from Rio—isolated by a wall, with barbed wire on top and guards at the entrance.*

Now Parvaneh's path meandered through a landscaped jungle, plants and trees lit by the soft pastel palette of ground lighting. I caught the glint of a fountain through a clearing in the trees, the view obscured by the arc of a footbridge. The surroundings were encapsulated by a fifteen-foot stone wall topped with concertina, and I looked to my right to locate the single structure I knew I'd find.

Precisely, Sage had replied. She seemed surprised that I guessed correctly. *But the garden perimeter is too heavily guarded...*

A set of stairs ascended a small hill, leading to a bamboo pavilion.

I'd only seen the pavilion once before, upon returning wounded from Rio. The Handler had stood there then, and at his feet was Ian, a bound captive.

On this night, I stood in the garden after an entire year on the perilous journey, traveling the world and narrowly escaping death in pursuit of vengeance against the Handler.

And now, for the first time, I had found a way.

* * *

Check out the next in series, Terminal Objective!
Continue reading for a sample.

Sign up for the Reader List and be the first to know about new releases and special offers from former Green Beret and USA Today bestselling author, Jason Kasper.

Join Jason Kasper's Reader List at Jason-Kasper.com

As a thank you for signing up, you'll receive a free copy of The Ranger Objective: An American Mercenary Short Story.

TERMINAL OBJECTIVE: AMERICAN MERCENARY #6

From the city streets of the US to the war-torn deserts of Africa. From the snow-capped mountains of Asia to the narco-controlled jungles of South America, forces have been fighting for control of the ultimate criminal empire.

When an act of violence plunges the contenders into a final confrontation, David Rivers is sent in. He's the first operative of a mercenary army.

Parachuting into Russia to link up with a mysterious intelligence agent, he must find a way to strike the heart of a ruthless criminal alliance.

The stakes couldn't be higher. If David doesn't succeed, he won't just lose his life—he'll lose everyone he cares about, too.

Because when this war is over, either one organization will stand...or none of them will.

Get your copy today at Jason-Kasper.com

ALSO BY JASON KASPER

American Mercenary Series

Greatest Enemy
Offer of Revenge
Dark Redemption
Vengeance Calling
The Suicide Cartel
Terminal Objective

Shadow Strike Series

The Enemies of My Country

Spider Heist Thrillers

The Spider Heist
The Sky Thieves

Want to stay in the loop?
Sign up to be the FIRST to learn about new releases. Plus get newsletter only bonus content for FREE.

As a thank you for signing up, you'll receive a free copy of *The Ranger Objective*. Join today at **Jason-Kasper.com/newsletter**

ACKNOWLEDGMENTS

I owe my heartfelt thanks to the following people for their help in creating *The Suicide Cartel*.

As always, Julie Napier worked tirelessly as content editor in revising the initial drafts.

Codename: Duchess and JT helped me revise the manuscript before sending it to my team of beta readers, who were instrumental in guiding my rewrites.

Beta readers for this book were: Bob Waterfield, (USN(SW) Ret.), Charlie Cabo, Dean Fukawa, Derek Burt, Dr. Earl, Gabi Rosetti, Jack Raburn (retired US military, 1969-93, Combat Veteran, Vietnam and Desert Storm), Jeane Jackson, Jim F, Jon Suttle, K4HJB, M Julien, Mike Rajkowski, MK, Ray Dennis, Tim Abbott, and Tim Clary.

A special thanks goes out to longtime David Rivers fan and beta reader extraordinaire, Joseph "Ishway" Iesué, who worked with me extensively on revising the first scene of the book.

My medical advisors were Bourbon Delta, Corey, and Randy. They deserve the credit for anything that Outfit medic Reilly did right while treating his casualty in the Triple Frontier.

Cara Quinlan not only provided her skillful professional editing services but also worked with me on fitting the manuscript into her schedule after I finished it much earlier than planned.

Finally, my beautiful and long-suffering wife Amy continues to make this all possible. Thanks to her continued support, I've been successfully dodging a day job for over two years of writing thriller novels. On behalf of myself, David Rivers, and all the readers who enjoy this series, THANK YOU!

ABOUT THE AUTHOR

Jason Kasper is the USA Today bestselling author of the Spider Heist, American Mercenary, and Shadow Strike thriller series. Before his writing career he served in the US Army, beginning as a Ranger private and ending as a Green Beret captain. Jason is a West Point graduate and a veteran of the Afghanistan and Iraq wars, and was an avid ultramarathon runner, skydiver, and BASE jumper, all of which inspire his fiction.

Never miss a new release! Sign up for the Reader List at Jason-Kasper.com/newsletter

Join the Facebook Reader Group for the latest updates: facebook.com/groups/JasonKasper

Contact info:
Jason-Kasper.com
Jason@Jason-Kasper.com

twitter.com/kasperauthor
instagram.com/kasperauthor

CPSIA information can be obtained
at www.ICGtesting.com
Printed in the USA
FSHW020724240520
70551FS